TALES OF ABUNUWAS

AND OTHER STORIES

RETOLD BY SUZI LEWIS-BARNED

MKUKI NA NYOTA

DAR – ES – SALAAM

Published by:
Mkuki na Nyota Publishers
P. O. Box 4246
Dar es Salaam
www.mkukinanyota.com

Illustrations by Abdul Gugu

ISBN 978-9987-08-043-4

Contents

Introduction

Hekaya za Abunuwas na Hadithi Nyingine is well known to most people throughout East Africa where Swahili is spoken, having for years been a Primary School reader. The stories, which are partly Arabic in origin, were first published in Swahili in 1935 by Macmillan & Co of London and later Nairobi, although their origin long predates that time. Of special interest are the delightful animal stories which are most likely to be pure African in origin. As far as is known, this is the first time these stories have been published in English.

Earlier editions state that the stories were told and written down by Africans and recorded in Swahili by a Reader of the International Languages Committee which was in the 1930s engaged in putting the language into Roman letters and numerals and standardising its spelling and grammar.

For those who are further interested, the names of some of those engaged in this work are recorded in the Preface of the Standard Swahili-English Dictionary by this Committee, published by Oxford University Press in 1939.

Tales of Abunuwas and other stories are based on translations from Swahili, *Hadithi za Abunuwas na Hadithi Nyingine*, into English by John Lewis-Barned and retold by his daughter Suzi. Abunuwas tales are, of course, available in English translations from the Arabic originals, but the translations into English from an early Swahili edition adds a new and interesting dimension. Abunuwas (or Abu Nawas) tales are loved by young and old readers alike throughout the world and on the East African coast which has had centuries old contacts with Arab traders and Islamic scholars "Hadithi za Abunuwasi" as they are called in Swahili have become an integral part of Swahili literature.

Abu Nawas, the nickname of their author, lived in Baghdad, Iraq, during the reign of Harun Al Rashid (763-809) and was considered the most accomplished Arab poet of his age. His tales spread far and wide in the Arab countries around the Mediterranean sea but also in Turkey, Uzbekistan and even beyond. Many of the tales appear also in the classic One Thousand and One Nights in which Harun Al Rashid is at the centre as the wise and just Sultan.

In addition to the Abunuwas tales, there are other stories, which come from the Swahili story telling tradition. These entertaining stories are full of gems of wisdom, ideas on justice and morality in day-to-day relations between people, between people and animals, and between animals and animals in a world in which brute force is pitted against cleverness and wit, which always triumphs.

The author, Suzi Lewis-Barned, now a freelance writer (www.lewis-barned.co.uk), is a former BBC researcher and journalist living near London. Suzi is also the author of The Clever Rat and other African Stories (Ragged Bears Publishing, 2002) another collection of African tales produced in collaboration with her father.

To my parents
John and Ursula
with love and thanks

Abunuwas Moves House

One day Abunuwas and his wife decided that their house was too small. They called round an Estate Agent, who advertised it for them in the local paper and in his shop, but for many months no one wanted to buy it.

Then one day the Estate Agent called round to say that someone was interested in buying just the top floor of the house. Reluctantly, Abunuwas agreed to sell it, and built a separate staircase which ran up the outside of the house. But when several more months passed and still no one wanted to buy the ground floor, Abunuwas tried to persuade the man upstairs to buy it. When he seemed reluctant, Abunuwas decided to play a trick on him.

He assembled a gang of workmen at the house and he called out to the man upstairs: "I'm going to demolish my house now and as it's underneath yours, you'd better hold tight in case your house tumbles down - and don't say I didn't warn you."

His neighbour was terrified and at once agreed to buy the rest of the house!

The Clever Thieves

Once upon a time there were two thieves who lived in a cave. One was called Daudi and he only stole during the day. The other was called Nguvu and he only stole by night. Although they both hid their loot in different parts of the same cave, they had never met.

One morning Daudi decided to take a walk down to the cave instead of going out to thieve as he usually did. When he arrived he was amazed to find Nguvu fast asleep there.

Daudi was sure that the sleeping man must be an informer and, holding a knife to his throat, he woke him roughly. Nguvu woke and, thinking that his misdeeds had been discovered, confessed immediately and then in a terrified, shaking voice promised: "I will never steal again."

"Are you a thief too?" asked Daudi, dropping the knife in surprise. "I don't believe you! Show me your takings". Nguvu took him to a deep part of the cave, which Daudi had never seen before, and showed him all the treasures he had stolen. The two thieves were astonished to learn from each other that they had been sharing the same cave for seven years, but had never met before. "This is amazing!" they said.

Daudi, the Day Thief, was very proud of his skill but he couldn't believe that Nguvu could be as talented a thief as he was. "I'll show you who's the best thief around here," he said. "Just watch me!"

Then Daudi rolled some clay into tiny balls like pearls and disguised himself to look like a smart merchant. He mounted a horse that he had stolen the day before, and rode up to the house of a very rich neighbour. "Have you any pearls you would like valued?" he asked. The rich man took out his collection and Daudi cleverly swapped his own clay imitations for the valuable pearls. Daudi took the pearls back to the cave and said to his friend, "There! See how clever I have been!"

But Nguvu, the Night Thief was not to be outdone. That evening he took twelve nails, a hammer and a knife and, dressed as a pauper, went to the Sultan's house. At first the guards at the gate refused to let him in but Nguvu told them a long story about how he had travelled many miles and had nowhere to stay. At last they agreed to let him sleep in the Court House for the night.

Nguvu slept until midnight, then he took
his knife, his hammer and his nails and,
while the striking of the church clock
drowned the noise of his hammer he
knocked the twelve nails into the wall of
the Sultan's house. Next he used the nails
as a ladder to climb up into the Sultan's
bedroom, where he and his wife – the
Sultana - were fast asleep. Nguvu stole
a gold chain from around the Sultana's
neck, as well as her diamond ring and
some money which he found hidden in a
large earthenware pot.

Then Nguvu climbed back down
his 'ladder' and ran back to the cave,
chanting, "Run, run, as fast as I can. They
can't catch me, I'm the Night Thief man!"

"Now look how clever I am!" he said to
Daudi when he reached the cave. "I often
steal from the Sultan but I have never had
such a rich haul as this!"

The two thieves marvelled at each other's
talents. "We make a great team," they
agreed. "If I steal at night and you steal
by day, we'll soon be offering a round-the-clock burglary service,"
laughed Nguvu.

When the Sultan and Sultana discovered that they had been robbed
they immediately gave orders that a hunt take place for the thief. They
ordered a 'curfew' which meant that anyone caught outside after 10
p.m. would be suspected of being a thief.

But this did not frighten Nguvu, the Night Thief. So, that night he waited until after the curfew and knocked loudly on the door of the village shop.

"What do you want?" asked the frightened shop keeper. "Don't you know there is a curfew?"

"Yes, but I am just a poor old man who has no oil for his lamp and I will give you twelve rupees if you will just let me have a drop to last until morning," lied Nguvu.

The offer of so much money was too much for the shop keeper who filled the lamp and held out his arm for the money. But the wicked Nguvu cut off his arm and ran off with it.

As he ran off, he chanted, "Run, run, as fast as I can. They can't catch me, I'm the Night Thief man!"

When he arrived back at the cave, Nguvu showed Daudi the arm. "See?" he said. "I'm not scared to do anything to get what I want!"

The next night Nguvu made some alcoholic bread, then disguised himself as a woman and left the cave carrying the loaves in a basket. It wasn't long before he was stopped by two policemen.

"Why are you out during the curfew?" they asked.

"I am going to the mosque to pray for the soul of my poor dead brother and to offer this bread as a sacrifice," replied Nguvu.

"Go home!" ordered the policemen, snatching away the bread. They ate it immediately for they had been patrolling the streets all night and they were very hungry. But the alcohol made them feel drunk and they very soon fell asleep.

Then Nguvu crept back and stole their guns and swords before racing back home, chanting, "Run, run, as fast as I can. They can't catch me, I'm the Night Thief man!"

When the Sultan heard that his policemen had been robbed, he was furious and was even more determined to catch the thieves.

The Sultan asked all the citizens for their help in catching the thieves. Posters were put up all over the town with a picture of Nguvu drawn by the policemen he had tricked, and the night curfew was enforced even more strictly than before.

One night the Sultan's Police Chief spotted Nguvu as he was coming out of a house he had been burgling, with some loot in a bag.

"Got you!" he shouted, grabbing Nguvu by the scruff of the neck, "You won't escape now. Give me your arm and I will make sure you never walk free again!"

But as the Police Chief fumbled in the dark for his handcuffs, Nguvu offered him the shopkeeper's severed arm which he swiftly handcuffed to his own. Meanwhile Nguvu ran speedily away, calling, "Run, run as fast as you can, you can't catch me, I'm the Night Thief man!"

The Police Chief was incensed by this mockery but also astonished at Nguvu's cheekiness. He ran to the Sultan's palace and told him how he had caught the thief red-handed. "How could you have been so foolish as to let him go?" asked the Sultan.

"He cut off his arm to escape me!" exclaimed the Police Chief.

"Well, at least he won't be difficult to catch now," said the Sultan. "We will search high and low for a thief with only one arm."

Of course it wasn't long before they found the one-armed shopkeeper who was seized and dragged out of his shop. "We've got you now and here's your arm to prove it!" said the Sultan triumphantly, holding out the grisly severed arm. But when the poor shopkeeper explained the terrible act of butchery which had befallen him, they realised that they had all once again been tricked by the wicked Night Thief.

The Sultan was by now determined to catch the thief himself. But when Nguvu heard of this he laughed until his sides ached. "They will never catch Nguvu the Night Thief," he said to himself.

That night Nguvu left his cave dressed in sacks and went to the house of a blind neighbour. He knocked on the door. "Is anyone home?" he called softly.

"Who are you?" asked the blind man.

"I am a poor man, and I am starving. Please give me some food," replied Nguvu.

"But have you not heard about the curfew?" asked the blind man.

"Why should I care about such things when you can see I am so weak

that I would beg from the Sultan himself," said the clever thief. "Please, if you cannot spare a morsel of food for me at least give me work to do so that I can earn some money."

So the blind man let him in and gave him some corn to grind. "Grind this corn until morning and I will give you sixpence," he said. But as he went up to bed, leaving Nguvu to grind the corn, he left the front door open, which was forbidden under the curfew rules.

The Sultan himself was passing the door and when he saw it was open, he asked Nguvu, "Who are you? And why is the front door wide open?"

"Why, pray, are you out in the middle of the night? Don't you know about the curfew?" replied Nguvu, side-stepping the Sultan's questions.

Then the Sultan said sharply, "That doesn't answer my question. Why is your door wide open?"

But Nguvu just replied, "Eh! great master, I fear for you wandering about at night. Have you not heard the Sultan's order?"

The Sultan said, "But that still does not answer my question. Tell me why your door is wide open when there is so much stealing in the town these days?"

Then the clever Nguvu replied, "It's terrible, isn't it? In fact, I saw a man pass the door a moment ago and he ran off that way". At once the Sultan ran off at high speed in the direction Nguvu had indicated. But, of course, he searched in vain and so he returned to Nguvu who was still pounding away at his corn.

"Did you catch him?" asked Nguvu.

"No," replied the Sultan.

"Listen!" said Nguvu, "I think I can hear the noise of a horse over there." So the Sultan again ran off after the 'thief' while Nguvu laughed to himself at the way he was tricking him. When he returned, Nguvu said, "This thief is playing 'cat and mouse' with you. He has just this minute come back this way and has gone off in that direction. But let us make a plan: why don't you let me put on your clothes and mount your horse while you put on my rags and grind this flour. Then if the thief returns he will not recognise you." And the foolish Sultan agreed to hand over his horse and his clothes to Nguvu and grind the flour. Nguvu immediately galloped off home on the Sultan's horse, trying to stay on it while he laughed and laughed at the way he had tricked him. Meanwhile the Sultan pounded away at the flour until daybreak waiting for Nguvu to return, which of course he didn't.

In the morning, the blind man woke up and was very cross because he could not see that the Sultan had taken Nguvu's place, and he had ground very little corn.

"You are no good!" shouted the blind man. "Where is the work you promised to do?

Have you sat here all night and done nothing?" Then he cuffed him and was about to inflict a second blow when the Sultan said,

"Don't you know who I am?"

"I do not," replied the blind man.

"I am the Sultan," he said.

The blind man was astonished. "Why did you come here seeking work last night?" he asked. Then the Sultan told him about Nguvu and what had happened. "We have both been tricked by this wicked man," said the blind man.

The Sultan was more angry than he had ever been in his life. "I am such a fool!" he said. "It is I who have acted like a blind man, not you." And he returned home more determined than ever to find Nguvu the Night Thief.

Some days later the people of the town gathered together and conducted a search party which discovered both the Day Thief and the Night Thief together in their cave. They were brought before the Sultan and condemned to prison for the rest of their lives.

The Cock and the Hare

Once upon a time a cock and a hare became friends. They visited each other often, even though they lived on opposite sides of the forest. As their friendship grew the cock started to let the hare in on some of his secrets, but he was never quite sure whether he could trust the hare to keep these secrets to himself. So one day he decided to test him.

Cock said to Hare: "It is important to me that I should be able to trust you with even my most precious secrets. Will you promise me that you will never tell anyone, even your wife, anything you hear while you are at my house?"

"Very well," replied Hare. "From now on I will not breathe a word of what you say to anyone else."

One day when Hare was coming to stay, Cock said to his wife: "Listen carefully to what I am going to tell you. In the middle of the night I will wake you up and say: 'It's time to cut off my head and put it on a plate.' You must reply: 'Bring me a sharp knife and I will cut it off immediately.' Then in the morning I will wake up, flap my wings and call: 'Bring me my head now and stick it back on again so that I can wake everyone up with my crowing' and you must reply: 'Why don't you just keep your head on when you go to sleep like everyone else?" Cock's wife agreed to do what he had said.

That afternoon Hare arrived at Cock's house and they chatted as usual until night fell. Then Cock said to Hare, "Do you remember that last time you stayed you promised not to repeat anything you heard said while you were here?"

"I do," replied Hare.

"Very well," said Cock, "Just remember to keep your promise. Good night."

"Sleep well, my friend," replied Hare.

Just as Hare was falling asleep he heard Cock cry out, "Wife! Wife! It's time to cut off my head and put it on a plate."

Cock's wife replied, "Bring me a sharp knife and I will cut it off immediately". Then she pretended to cut off her husband's head, saying. "Sleep well now, and wake bright and early."

The hare, who had of course overheard the conversation, was amazed. But he was even more amazed when at dawn he heard the cock calling to his wife, "Wife! Wife! Bring me my head now and stick it back on again so that I can wake everyone up with my crowing." A short time afterwards, Hare heard Cock crowing as usual.

After several days, during which Hare overheard the same conversation between Cock and his wife every night and morning, the time came for him to leave. He bid Cock and his wife a fond farewell and set off across the forest. But he was so amazed by what had happened that when he arrived home, he forgot his promise and immediately told his wife all that had happened. "Perhaps I should try it," he said to his wife.

"It sounds a crazy idea," she replied. But the more he thought about it, the more Hare was sure that if Cock slept better that way, then so would he.

When Cock came to stay with him a few weeks later, Hare decided to try out this new way of sleeping. When it was time for bed Cock went to bed, but just as he was about to doze off he overheard Hare saying, "It's time to cut off my head and put it on a plate." Then he heard the sound of Hare's wife cutting off his head while Hare screamed out in pain, and he knew his friend had not kept his promise. Hare's wife tried to put his head back on, but it was no use.

Then Cock sadly told her of what he had done to test his friend Hare. "I made up a story to test whether my friend Hare could be trusted and I am sad that he could not," he said. And so they buried the hare and Cock returned sadly home.

Abunuwas and the Donkey

One day Abunuwas found that he had saved enough gold coins to buy a donkey. So he went to the market and bought the finest donkey there was. Then he got on it and rode home.

The next day a man called wanting to borrow the donkey. Abunuwas, who didn't want to lend his donkey to the man, said "The donkey is not here." But just at that moment the donkey brayed.

The man said "How come I can hear
a donkey braying yet you say he is not
here?"

Abunuwas replied "Have you come to
borrow a donkey or a donkey's bray?"
Then he started to bray himself, and
laughed: "Come on now, mount if you
will and go whence you came!"

Fikirini and Hemedi

Long ago in the land of Pate lived a Master Tailor who owned a large shop with twenty apprentices. Amongst them was one called Fikirini.

Fikirini was very good at his job, but he was also very vain and he liked to imagine that he was very grand. He made friends with the sons of Sultans, not because he liked them, but because they were powerful and important. He began to dress like them, with much finery and silk and when people greeted him he acknowledged them by touching his head with his hand just as Sultans do.

As time went by Fikirini became so convinced of his own importance that he began to believe he would make a better Sultan's son than any of his friends.

One day the Master Tailor asked Fikirini to mend a Sultan's robe. Fikirini worked late to finish it, and when all the other apprentices had gone home, he put it on, looked in the mirror and struck his most Sultanly pose. "This is indeed my lucky day," he said to himself, "Now I shall truly be the son of a Sultan."

That night Fikirini left the land of Pate to seek his fortune dressed in the Sultan's robe, and he looked so like a Sultan's son that everyone he met along the road bowed down before him. After he'd been travelling for a few days, Fikirini met a real Sultan's son, whose name was Hemedi.

"Hello," said Fikirini. "Where are you going?"

"I don't know," said Hemedi. "I am feeling very confused. What about you?"

"I'm not sure either," said Fikirini. So

they tied up their horses, got out their food, and sat down for a long chat.

"Tell me your story," said Fikirini to Hemedi.

"Well, until last week I thought I was the son of the Sultan of Guba," began Hemedi. "He brought me up as his son but a few days ago, on my twenty-first birthday, he told me that I'm really the son of the great Sultan of Baghdad."

"How come?" asked Fikirini.

"On the day I was born some wise men came to see my father and told him that he should send me away because some evil men were planning to kill me. They told him that I should not return to my father's kingdom for twenty-one years," explained Hemedi.

"But after all that time, how will your father know you are his son?" asked Fikirini.

"When he left me with the Sultan of Guba he gave him this dagger for me to bring back so he will know I am truly his son," explained Hemedi.

Then Fikirini told Hemedi about his ambition to be rich and powerful. "I may only be an apprentice tailor, but I know I am destined for better things," he said. Hemedi promised to help him become the most rich and famous tailor in Baghdad when he became the Sultan.

But after Hemedi had gone to sleep that night, Fikirini stole his dagger and his horse and set off for Baghdad. He galloped up to the palace gates and shouted, "I am Hemedi, the son of the Sultan!" And the guards rushed to tell Hemedi's father, the old Sultan.

Fikirini took Hemedi's dagger from its sheath and handed it to the old man, who hugged him and said, "Praise be to God, who has brought my precious son home to me. Let there be a great feast in his honour, and much rejoicing."

Then all the people shouted, "Hemedi has come home! Hemedi has come home! Praise be to God!"

The Sultan took Fikirini into the palace. "Come and see your mother," he said. But Fikirini held back.

"There's something I have to tell you first," he said. "While I was making my way home I met an imposter who claims to be your son, but he's really just a tailor's apprentice."

"Indeed," replied the Sultan. Then he led the way to the palace, where his wife had already heard of her son's arrival.

"Go on in and greet your mother," said the Sultan.

But when she saw Fikirini, the Sultan's wife said, "This is not my son. I may not have seen him since he was a baby, but a mother knows her own son - and this is not he."

Just then Hemedi, who had woken to find Fikirini and his horse gone, and had followed behind him as quickly as he could, rushed into the palace, shouting, "Mother, it is I! Please believe me! This imposter is just a common tailor's apprentice!" The Sultan, who believed what Fikirini had told him, ordered Hemedi to be thrown in the dungeons.

But when the Sultan's wife saw Hemedi, she was convinced that he was indeed her son. "I have a plan which will prove to you which of the two men is our son," she said to her husband.

The next morning the two young men were summoned before the Sultan and Sultana. They were each ordered to make a cloak, fit for the Sultan himself.

Fikirini knew that to make the cloak would be easy for him. "I shall make a cloak that will fill everyone with wonder," he said. But Hemedi was lost for words, because he'd never even sewn on a button before. Fikirini made a really beautiful cloak, but Hemedi didn't even cut out the cloth.

"Why have you not done as I ordered?" roared the Sultan.

"I don't know how to cut cloth, because Sultans' sons have tailors to sew for them," replied his son.

Now the Sultana was convinced he was her son, but the Sultan decided
to put the pair to a final test, just to be certain. He had two boxes
made. On the top of the first box, which was encrusted with pearls,
was inscribed: "I Seek Wealth and Fortune" and on the other, a plain
wooden box, "I Honour My Country".

The Sultan summoned a great assembly of people and arranged for the
boxes to be placed on a table. Then he called Fikirini and Hemedi and
asked them to choose a box each. When Fikirini chose the box with "I
Seek Wealth and Fortune" inscribed on it, and Hemedi chose "I Honour
My Country" the Sultan knew at last that he was indeed his son, for the
son of a Sultan has no need to seek wealth or fortune.

So the Sultan called Fikirini and Hemedi and gave them each the boxes
they had chosen. In Fikirini's box there was a needle and thread but in
Hemedi's box there was a crown.

Then the Sultan crowned Hemedi, and he reigned as Sultan of
Baghdad for many years. But Fikirini was chased out of the land
clutching his box and was never seen again.

Abunuwas and the Saucepan

One day Abunuwas's donkey was very thirsty but Abunuwas had no bowl from which he could drink. So he went to his neighbour and asked: "Please may I borrow a bowl so I can give my donkey a drink?" And his neighbour lent him a brass saucepan which Abunuwas kept for three days.

On the fourth day, Abunuwas returned the saucepan to the owner, together with a very small saucepan which he put inside it.

"Here is your saucepan," he said.

The owner looked inside and said, "This little saucepan is not mine."

But Abunuwas replied, "I cannot steal other people's property; your saucepan gave birth whilst with me and this is the baby."

At this his neighbour was overjoyed, declaring: "How amazing! Your house must be magic if saucepans can give birth there."

Three days later, Abunuwas went back to borrow the saucepan again. But this time he kept it and when the owner asked for it back, he said, "Your saucepan has died."

The owner looked puzzled and asked, "How can a brass saucepan die?"

Abunuwas laughingly replied, "Everything that gives birth must eventually die."

The owner was amazed. But however many scholars he consulted on the subject, they all confirmed that those who are born must surely die. And so Abunuwas kept the saucepan!

Hamadi's Daughters

There was once a man called Hamadi who had seven beautiful daughters. But Hamadi was a wise man, and wise men have many enemies. One of these was Joram, a local merchant who had once been made to look foolish by Hamadi in front of his friends when he was a young boy. Although Hamadi did not know it, Joram was an evil man who was determined to wreak revenge on him.

Over the years, Joram became very rich, so when he proposed to Hamadi's eldest daughter, Asha, it was hard for Hamadi, who was very poor, to refuse him although he knew in his heart that Joram was not a good man. And he was right. Joram did not marry Asha because he loved her, he married her to punish her father.

As soon as they were married, Joram shut Asha up in a house with many servants, but he did not allow her any food. Each day, Joram went to his father's house to eat, taking the servants with him but poor Asha was left to starve. Joram did not allow her to visit her family, and in those days there were no telephones, so she was not able to tell them how badly Joram was treating her. Asha became weaker and weaker until she died of starvation.

Then Joram went to Hamadi and pretended to be heartbroken. He told Hamadi that Asha had been taken ill and had died suddenly.

Joram believed him, and promised to allow him to marry Asha's younger sister, Saida.

But Joram treated his second wife in exactly the same way as his first and it wasn't long before she, too, had been starved to death. Again Hamadi believed what Joram told him and allowed him to marry another of the sisters and the sad story was repeated until six out of the seven daughters had died.

But when it came to Hamadi's youngest daughter, Anania, Joram had quite a surprise for she was much wiser than her sisters and when she arrived at her new home and realised the terrible things that had happened to her sisters, she decided to outwit her evil husband.

Whenever Joram went out of the house, Anania managed to slip out too. She would dash back to her father's house and eat as much as she could before returning to the house. She pretended that she had never left the house and Joram was very surprised that she remained so plump and healthy.

One night, when Joram had been out and had returned to find Anania happily making a dress for herself, he asked her, "How is it that you never eat, and yet you seem to be so healthy?"

"Did my father not tell you that I am a sorceress?" asked Anania.

Joram was terrified. "What kind of sorceress?" he asked her.

"The kind of sorceress who knows what an evil man you are," she replied.

Joram shook with fear and fell down on his knees in front of his wife. "Please spare me," he begged.

"It is too late," she replied. "If you do not go to my father and tell him the truth about my sisters, you will die a most horrible death."

Joram was so frightened that he rushed to Hamadi immediately and confessed to his wrong doings. Hamadi immediately called the Sultan who had him arrested and put in prison. So Anania and her family were able to live happily ever after.

Abunuwas and the Kite

It was unfortunate for Abunuwas that he had enemies in the town of Baghdad. Some important people wanted to make trouble for him with the Sultan and have him killed. When he asked the Sultan if there was anything he could do to save his life, the Sultan ordered him to go and build a house high in the sky within three days, or he would be killed.

Abunuwas was puzzled, but he could not disobey the Sultan so he decided instead to outwit him. He said, "I hear you Sultan. It shall be done." Abunuwas made some paper out of wood and glued it together with arrowroot glue to make a huge kite. On it he put a bell which he tied with a piece of rope to a tree. And when all the people saw this kite in the air and heard the bell tinkling, they were astonished because they had never seen anything like it before.

Then Abunuwas went back to the Sultan and said, "I have done as you said, Great Master. Look out of the window and you will see for yourself." The Sultan opened his window and Abunuwas pointed to the kite. "Do you see it up there?" he asked.

"I do," replied the Sultan.

"Do you hear the noise?" said Abunuwas, as the wind made the kite dance around.

"I do," replied the Sultan.

"That noise you hear is of the hammers of the carpenters who are nailing down the floor, but they are a bit short of planks. Would you do me the kindness of supplying me with some planks and some men to carry them?" asked Abunuwas.

"Certainly, but how will the men reach it?" asked the Sultan.

"The same way as I do," said Abunuwas.

So the Sultan said to his workmen, "Take these planks and follow Abunuwas."

Abunuwas took the men to the place where he had tied the kite up with rope and said, "This is the way, up you go."

The men were terrified. "We can't balance on that rope," they said. But Abunuwas replied, "There is no other way." The men discussed the problem over their lunch and decided that Abunuwas must be crazy. Then they went back to him and insisted, "We can't do it."

"Then you must go and see your master," said Abunuwas.

The labourers returned to the Sultan and told him, "We can't climb that rope with these planks."

And the Sultan answered, "Indeed, no man could climb a rope like that."

Then Abunuwas, who had followed them, asked: "Then why did you tell me to build a house in the sky?"

And the Sultan was dumbfounded and could not answer. So Abunuwas went and cut the rope which held the kite which flew away, as kites do.

The Tale of the Chicken and the Hawk

Long ago there was a hawk who had only one son. However, his son became ill and it seemed he would die, so the old hawk called together all the animals of the forest, hoping they might know how to make his son better.

Among the animals there was a cunning chicken. He thought of a plan to cheat the hawk out of some money and make a feast for his own family. He went to the hawk and told him that he knew a spider who would make his son well, but only if he paid fifty gold coins first. The hawk willingly handed over the money, trusting the chicken to do as he had promised.

The chicken hurried off to the spider's house. "Spider!" he shouted.

"What do you want?" asked the spider warily.

"I know that you are a very clever doctor," said the chicken, "and I have come to ask you to make the hawk's son better."

"How do I know you will not eat me?" asked the spider.

"Why should I eat you?" asked the chicken, licking his lips because he knew the spider was big and juicy. "Look out of your window and I will show you the fifty gold coins I have for you."

The spider looked out of the window and saw the coins and he was foolish enough to believe what the chicken had said. He opened the door, clutching his medicine bag, and set off with the spider to Hawk's house.

When they had walked about halfway, Chicken and his family leapt upon Spider and killed him. After they had eaten him, they took out the medicines from Spider's bag, broke the bottles, and poured the contents all over the ground. Meanwhile the hawk waited and waited for Chicken to return with Spider in vain. With great sadness, he watched his son grow weaker and weaker until he died. Then he took a stout stick and set off along the road to see what had happened.

When he came upon the broken bottles strewn across the road and the spider's clothes lying there he stopped. He looked inside the medicine bag and found a letter addressed to him. It said: "Chicken came to tell me your son was very sick so I am hurrying to your house in time to save his life."

When the hawk read the letter and saw the confusion around him, he realised what the chicken had done and he asked himself how he could get even. Then he told everyone – including man and all the animals - that if they ever met a chicken or its chicks they should kill them without pity and eat them.

And so from that time onwards the hawk and the chicken became enemies and even today you can hear the hawk wail for the loss of his son as he looks for chicks to seize and kill in revenge.

Abunuwas and the Poor Couple

Once there lived a poor old man and his wife. They were always hungry because they could never afford to buy enough food.

One day a rich young man, who was passing through their village with a group of friends, decided to play a cruel joke on the man. "Watch this," he said to his friends. "We'll make this old man look a complete fool."

He said to the old man: "If you can spend all night in that frozen pond, I will give you ten thousand gold pieces." The old man reluctantly agreed to accept the challenge but his wife, who was very worried about him, went with him, bringing a burning torch so that he could see some light and have some company. While the rich young men drank their wine and made merry by the fireside on the other side of the pond, the old man shivered and shook, but managed to stay alive.

The next morning the poor old man begged the rich young man to pay him the ten thousand gold pieces, but the rich man refused - Why won't you pay me?" asked the poor old man.

"Your wife kept you warm with a burning torch," said the rich young man.

"The torch was far from me, and all it gave me was light," said the old man. But still the rich young man refused to hand over the money.

The old man and his wife went to see the wise Abunuwas and asked for his help. "If you will pay me three thousand of the ten thousand gold pieces you are given, I will work out a way to get your money," said Abunuwas. The old man agreed.

Then Abunuwas told the old man to go and tell the Sultan everything that had happened. But the rich young man argued his side of the story so well that the Sultan believed that the torch had indeed warmed the old man and said that he did not deserve the ten thousand gold coins.

The old man went back to Abunuwas in despair and told him what had happened. But Abunuwas said, "Don't worry - I have a plan. One way or another you will get your money."

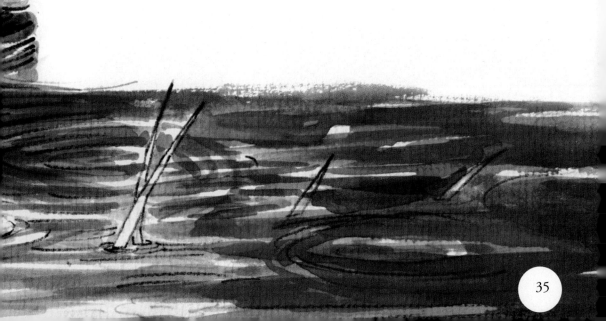

Abunuwas brought enough food to make a sumptuous feast, to which he invited the Sultan and his attendants. In one part of his kitchen he lit a fire and in another part he put together all the ingredients in a pan ready to be cooked.

The Sultan and the other guests waited all evening for their food but there was not even the faintest whiff of cooking. Towards the end of the evening the Sultan popped his nose round the door of the kitchen, where Abunuwas was supposed to be preparing the feast and he saw that the food was not being cooked at all. He said to Abunuwas, "Why have you invited us all for a feast but not cooked it yet?"

Abunuwas replied: "The food is cooking."

"It will never cook if it is so far from the fire," said the Sultan. And he added: "I always thought you were a wise man, but now I can see you are very stupid."

But Abunuwas replied, "Great master, don't be angry. Do you remember the poor old man who spend the night in a cold water of a pond, and who brought the matter to your court recently?"

"I do," replied the Sultan.

"You believed the rich young man who told you that the burning torch his wife brought with her had warmed the poor old man up, but it was as far from him as this meat is from the fire. Tell me, how could he have got any warmth from that? Please reconsider your decision and make the rich young man give him the money he agreed to pay."

The Sultan thought for a moment. "Yes, I can see now that you must be right," he said. And he went to the rich young man and ordered that he should hand over the ten thousand gold coins immediately.

The Clever Poor Man

In a village at the foot of a high mountain, there lived a poor old man called Hamedi. He had no children to look after him and he was too old to work in the fields. He lived in an old cottage and had little to eat. But he was a clever old man, and one day he thought of a plan to make himself rich.

One morning Hamedi set off along the road to the Sultan's palace and pleaded for an audience with him in private. The Sultan, who had a few minutes to spare, agreed and showed him into one of his chambers. "What do you want?" asked the Sultan.

"Oh! great Sultan, I have come to you seeking work, but I want no wages, nor food nor clothing," said Hamedi. "I just want one promise from you."

"Very well," replied the Sultan. "What would you like me to promise?"
"When you hold court I want you to invite me, together with your councillors, and from time to time I would like you to whisper in my ear," he replied.

"What shall I say to you?" asked the Sultan.

"Whatever you like, Great Master," replied Hamedi. "You can even insult me if you like. But let it be only me who hears what you whisper."

"Very well," agreed the Sultan. And so it was that each day old Hamedi came to the courthouse which was full of the Sultan's advisors. And he sat next to the Sultan who would lean over and whisper the most terrible insults in his ear whenever the mood took him. And all that Hamedi said in reply was, "Yes, Master."

But the Elders were baffled by these exchanges. After all, they had worked for years, trying to please the Sultan in any way they could. And now, here was this old man who appeared to be sharing secrets with their master. They were irritated at his favoured position but they also saw that such a close friend of the Sultan might be useful.

One day the most senior councillor invited Hamedi to his house for dinner. Then he asked him, "Why does the Sultan invite you, a poor old man, to all the council meetings, and why does he keep whispering in your ear?"

"The Sultan consults me about many matters," replied Hamedi. "In fact, he discussed with me only today the merits of your work and whether or not you should be dismissed. But I told him, "This councillor is very good and if he were to leave you would not find another like him anywhere.""

The councillor was very pleased and handed Hamedi a great deal of money before he left.

The next day Hamedi was invited to the home of another councillor where he was asked the same questions and he gave the same replies, and this continued until he had been to the homes of all the Sultan's advisors and had collected together a great deal of money.

The morning after he had been entertained by the last of the Sultan's advisors, Hamedi took his bag of money and moved far away from the Sultan's kingdom to another village where he lived happily and comfortably for the rest of his days.

Abunuwas and the Lions

Abunuwas was a wise man, but wise men are not always popular. One day some bad men whom Abunuwas had got the better of on several occasions thought of a plan to get rid of him once and for all. They went to see the Sultan of Baghdad, where they lived, who was called Harun Raschid and told him many lies about Abunuwas, claiming that he had harmed people and was a dangerous man who should be put to death.

The lies were so convincing that eventually Harun Raschid ordered Abunuwas to be thrown to the lions. But Abunuwas was too clever to be killed: he scratched, tickled, and stroked the lions who thought it was such fun that they decided not to eat him. Abunuwas even taught them some simple tricks. For instance, if he pointed his finger at someone, they would chase whoever was in the direction it was pointing.

Abunuwas and the lions shared the meat which was thrown to them each day and the rest of the townsfolk marvelled at his skill in taming these fierce beasts.

One morning something very strange happened. The people of Baghdad saw an arm reaching out of the sea, with three fingers outstretched. They paddled out and tried to pull out whoever the arm belonged to, but their hands just passed through it. "It must be a sign," they said. But even the wisest scholars of the town could not work out what this sign meant. After a time the people became very scared. "Perhaps this is something to do with Abunuwas," they said. "Perhaps it is a sign that he must be released." They decided to let Abunuwas out of the lion pit to see if he could tell them what the strange arm could mean.

Abunuwas went to the edge of the water and looked at the arm, which was now holding up three fingers.

"What does it mean?" asked the people. "It means that there are three things to be done," replied Abunuwas, who really had no idea what the fingers meant but had thought of a cunning plan to be set free.

"Tell us what to do," demanded the Sultan, convinced now of Abunuwas' wisdom.

"First, we must let the lions decide who is evil," said Abunuwas. He went to the pit and let out the lions, pointing his fingers at all the men who had told lies about him. The lions chased them away, eating a few of them as they went, and then returned to roll around at Abunuwas' feet while he tickled their tummies.

"Now what must we do?" asked Harun Raschid.

"The second thing we must do is to build a wall around the city to keep out our enemies, and then you, O Sultan, need to choose the wisest of men to help you make decisions," said Abunuwas.

The Sultan had the wall built and chose Abunuwas as the wisest of men. Then he had a fine palace built for him with the lions at the gate to guard it.

Shortly afterwards the arm disappeared and was never seen again, which was lucky for Abunuwas, wasn't it? Some months later the Sultan had a strange dream. He dreamed that under the palace he had built for Abunuwas there was a chest full of gold coins. Believing his dream to be true, he sent some workmen to dig under the house while Abunuwas was out. Abunuwas was very annoyed about this, especially as the workmen found nothing. "I will pay Harun Rashid back for this," he said to himself.

He cooked a meal of rice and meat, then left it uncovered on his kitchen table while he went out. When he came back some flies had settled on it and had started to eat it. Abunuwas covered them with a cloth and took the plate to the Sultan. "I want these flies prosecuted for eating my lunch," said Abunuwas.

"Prosecute flies?" asked the Sultan incredulously. "Why?"

"They have stolen my food and must be punished," said Abunuwas.

"But how can I prosecute flies?" asked the Sultan.

"I don't know but they must be judged according to the law," said Abunuwas.

"Very well," said Harun Raschid, the Sultan. "I give you permission to swat any fly you see."

"I'd like you to write that down please," said Abunuwas. So the Sultan gave Abunuwas written permission to swat any fly he saw. Now I will have my revenge, thought Abunuwas. He also decided to get his own back on the townsfolk who had persuaded the Sultan to throw him to the lions.

So Abunuwas made a large swat and whenever he passed a shop

and saw flies on the food he swatted them, causing chaos as the food flew around everywhere. When he saw flies on the dates at a market stall, he beat the dates and sent them flying; when he saw flies on the dried shark at another stall, he beat it until it flew into the air. The shopkeepers were furious at having their food treated this way but Abunuwas showed them his written warrant and they could not argue with him.

Finally, he went to the courthouse with his swat. He sat next to Harun Raschid, the Sultan, and when he saw a fly settle on his nose, he swatted it with all his might.

The Sultan fell to the ground, there was uproar in the court and the guards seized Abunuwas, intending to throw him in prison. But Abunuwas cried out: "If you lock me up you are persecuting me. I did not strike the Sultan deliberately; I was trying to protect him by hitting the fly on his nose. Look at this paper and you will see that he has given me permission to swat any fly I see." So the document was examined and seen to be authentic, and Abunuwas was released. As he ambled home, he laughed to himself because once more he had proved himself to be a clever man.

The Tale of the Hare
and the Mongoose

Long, long ago, a mongoose and a hare became friends and decided to live together and share their food one with another.

One day when they were out hunting they came upon some guinea fowl eggs. "Yum, yum!" said Mongoose. "I just adore eating guinea fowl eggs."

"Let's trap the guinea fowl too while we're about it," said Hare. So they set a trap and caught the guinea fowl which they took home for supper.

Then Hare said to Mongoose, "My friend I am feeling very tired after all that hunting. I'm going to take a nap."

"All right," said Mongoose, "I will cook supper while you sleep."

While Mongoose was cooking the guineafowl and its eggs, Hare fell asleep. But Mongoose didn't wake him to share the food and ate it all up. Then he hid the egg shells, threw the feathers in the fire and pretended to go to sleep.

The smell of the burning feathers woke Hare up with a start. "Where is the guineafowl, my friend?" he asked Mongoose.

"Oh no!" exclaimed Mongoose, pretending to be surprised. "I left it cooking here on the fire but it seems to have burnt away."

"Never mind," said Hare, pretending to believe him although he could smell the food on Mongoose's breath. "We all make mistakes. Well, I suppose I'd better go and look for something else for us to eat."

The Mongoose, whose tummy was of course full, settled down to sleep while Hare pretended to go off hunting.

When Mongoose was sound asleep, Hare took some banana leaves and tied him up with them so that he could not see or move. Then he took a stick and beat him hard until he begged for mercy. Then Hare ran off, leaving Mongoose wailing with pain.

When Hare returned he gently prodded Mongoose with his paw. "What's going on here?" he asked.

"It is I, your friend Mongoose," replied Mongoose.

"What on earth has happened to you?" asked Hare, pretending to be surprised.

"Someone tied me up in banana leaves and beat me," wailed Mongoose.

"How terrible," replied Hare, smiling to himself.

One morning a few days later, Mongoose got up early, before Hare had awoken, to hunt a beautiful bird called the *Kiumbizi* which he had spotted nesting in the branches of a nearby tree. He dressed himself up in his hunting clothes and stuck guinea fowl feathers and egg shells on his head. Then, feeling very smart and pleased with himself, he set off to chase the *Kiumbizi*.

When Hare awoke, he heard the sound of a flute piping a merry tune. He crept to a clearing in the bush and saw Mongoose chasing after the Kiumbizi bird, alternately piping and singing:-

'I'm going to catch the Kiumbizi bird
Just like I caught the Guinea fowl — you heard?
Eat it up and burn its bones in the fire.

Nice full tummy!
Yum! Yum! Yummy!"

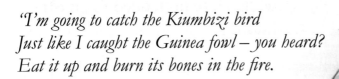

When Hare heard this, he took a drum
and beat it, singing:

"I caught the thief and I tied him up
With the leaves of the banana tree
Then I beat him soundly
Serves him right!
Ha! Ha! Ha! Hee! Hee! Hee!"

Then there was silence. At first the Mongoose
did not understand what he was hearing, but
when he realised how Hare had paid him back
for his trickery, he seized a stick and the two
friends began to fight. And ever since then
the Hare and the Mongoose have been the
greatest of enemies.

49

The Rich Man and the Poor Man

Once upon a time a rich man was barbecuing some goat's meat to eat for his supper. While it was cooking, there was a most delicious smell wafting around in the air. A poor man, who was passing by with his own food, sat down to eat on the windward side so that the smell of the cooking would make his own meagre rice supper taste better.

The next morning the poor man went to the rich man and said: "Sir, you have done a poor man a favour. Your supper last night smelt so delicious it made my food taste much better."

"Ah," replied the rich man. "That's why my meat didn't taste as good as usual. You smelt away some of its flavour, didn't you? You'll pay for this." And he took the poor man to the Court of the Sultan, Harun Raschid, where he was ordered to pay the rich man a fine of twelve gold coins.

The poor man went home to his wife and wept because they had no money to pay the fine.

"Why don't you go and see our friend, the wise Abunuwas, and ask his advice? I'm sure he will be able to help us," said his wife.

Abunuwas was sitting in his mud hut, surrounded by his children and his grandchildren, and he listened carefully to the poor man's story.

aThen he sat silently thinking for a few minutes. Finally he handed the poor man twelve gold coins.

"Here you are," he said. "Take these to the Court of the Sultan but don't hand them over until I arrive." In the morning the poor man arrived at the Sultan's Court with the twelve gold coins in his moneybag. He begged the Sultan to let him off the debt because, after all, he had not eaten the meat, only smelt it. But the Sultan insisted that the money be paid.

Just then Abunuwas arrived. "Open your money bag," he said. The poor man reluctantly opened his bag. Then Abunuwas took the money and threw it down on the ground. But as the rich man bent down to pick it up, Abunuwas shouted, "Wait! You can only take the jingle of these away with you, not the coins, because this man only sniffed your meat, he didn't eat it."

The Sultan was so dumbfounded by Abunuwas's argument that he allowed the poor man to leave, still clutching his coins. And there are many other stories of the wise Abunuwas but I'll tell you those another day...

The Tale of the Mgindo Girl

A long time ago there lived an old woman who had only one daughter, whose name was Asha. She was a beautiful girl, and many men had asked her to marry them but she had always said no, and this is why:

The old woman, whose name was Shaba, had told Asha never to agree to marry without asking her first. The reason for this was that she was getting older and found it harder to see, so she wanted to make sure that whoever Asha married would look after her as well as her daughter.

Early one morning, when her mother was out feeding the chickens, Asha heard a knock at the door. Outside was a handsome young man, surrounded by a group of his friends who were laughing and joking with one another.

"What do you want?" asked Asha.

"I have come to ask you to marry me," answered the handsome young man.

"Wait a moment while I go and fetch Mother," said Asha and she went round to the back of the house, calling, "Mother, mother, we have some visitors, and one of them has asked me to marry him."

Then Shaba said to her daughter, "You go ahead of me and offer them a drink, and I will catch up with you." Then she put on some old rags and bound up her knee as if it had been injured. She limped slowly after her daughter and when she got near the house she began to cry out in pain and stumble up the path. As she hobbled along, she called out:

*"My back is bent
I'm all but spent
And where's my daughter gone?"*

Now when the handsome young man and his friends saw the old lady hobbling and wobbling, falling over and trying to call out all at the same time, they fell about laughing at her. When she finally stumbled through the door to the house, she asked the young man what he wanted.

"I have come to ask if I may marry your daughter," said the handsome young man.

But the old widow replied, "I may be almost blind but I can see that you have no kindness in your heart. My daughter has no need of a husband like you." And she sent the young man and his friends away.

Some months later, Asha was excited to see the Sultan's son coming up the path, followed by a procession of courtiers bearing gifts for her. She rushed to find her mother, who again put on some old rags and bound up her knee as if it had been injured. Then she hobbled up the path, singing out:

"My back is bent
I'm all but spent
And where's my daughter gone?"

As she approached the house the Sultan's son could not help laughing at her, and he asked Asha, "Do you know who that mad old woman is?"

Asha showed him into the house and soon Shaba joined them. When Shaba asked him why he had come, the Sultan's son explained that he wished to marry her daughter. He was so polite that she found it hard to believe that it was he whom she had heard laughing at her as she hobbled up the path. "I may be almost blind, but I can see that you have no kindness in your heart. My daughter has no need of a husband like you," she said. And she sent the Sultan's son away.

54

After several more months, and countless more visits from young men who were all found to be unkind, Asha finally saw the son of the Chief Minister of State coming up the path. Once more he was invited in by Asha and once more her mother came hobbling up the path, singing out:

"My back is bent
I'm all but spent
And where's my daughter gone?"

The young man was horrified. He rushed to help her, and gently took her arm, asking, "Are you all right now?" When he realised that she was almost blind, he said, "How terrible for you. Is there anything I can do to help you?"

"Why have you come to see me?" asked Shaba.

"I came to ask whether I might marry your daughter," he replied.

"You have great kindness in your heart," replied the old widow. "Look Asha, this man has been gentle with me and this is how he will be with you."

And so it was that Asha came to be happily married and the old lady was cared for with great tenderness for the rest of her days.

The Man From the Next World

Long ago there lived a man, his wife, and their daughter. They were very poor and had only one cow for milk, and a small *shamba* (plot) on which to grow their food. The man left early each morning to work in the fields, collecting food for the cow on his way home.

One night the daughter had a dream that she had grown up into a beautiful woman with a baby of her own. The next morning, after her father had left for work, her mother found her weeping and wailing inconsolably. "Whatever is the matter?" she asked.

"I have lost my baby," cried the little girl. "I dreamed that I had a beautiful little girl but now that I have woken up she is no longer here."

"That's terrible," said her mother and she too burst into loud weeping and wailing, so the air was filled with the terrible noise they were making. Soon all the neighbours gathered round to find out what was the matter and when the foolish women told them, they roared with laughter.

"How ridiculous!" they said. "We have never in all our lives heard such a fuss about a dream." But the mother and her daughter just continued to weep and wail loudly.

After a while the terrible noise began to annoy everyone. So the neighbours got together and thought up a clever plan to quieten the pair and have a party at the same time. "If you don't cheer your little girl up, she will die of grief," they said.

"What shall I do?" wept the distraught mother.

"You could throw a party - that would make her happy," said the neighbours. And they persuaded her to let them kill the cow and prepare a great feast for the village.

Later that evening the husband came back from work. When he heard what had happened he could hardly believe his ears. "In all my life I do not think I have ever met such a fool as you," he said to his wife. "How could you kill our only cow just because of a dream? I am leaving you. If I ever find anyone as foolish as you I will come back,

but if not you will never see me again." And off he went, leaving his wife and daughter weeping and wailing more loudly than ever.

While he travelled the husband thought of ways to discover if there was anyone in the world more foolish than his wife. After a few days he came to a large town where he met a Wise Woman. He asked her: "Who is the most foolish person you know?"

"The Sultan is a fool - but his wife is even more foolish - she believes anything anyone tells her," replied the Wise Woman. Then the man sat down to think of a plan to discover for himself whether the Sultana was indeed as foolish as his own wife.

The next morning the man wrote a letter which he carefully folded and put into an envelope before asking the Wise Woman for directions to the house of the Sultana.

When he got there he saw a pile of lime near the window of the house. And he dug down into the lime and covered himself in it so it flew about like smoke around his head, and then he shouted, "Help me! Help me, someone!"

The Sultana put her head out of the window and shouted down: "Who are you?"

"I am a messenger from the next world," replied the man. "I have a letter to deliver to the Sultan's wife."

"Give it to me," ordered the Sultana, and she read the letter which went as follows:

'Greetings, oh beloved Niece. All is well in the next world and all your relations here are well but I am saddled with debt. I have borrowed some money but I have nothing left to repay my debtors. Please give a thousand gold coins to the messenger who gave you this letter so I can repay my debt. Greetings! signed, Your Uncle'.

When the Sultan's wife read the letter she was very sad and she went straight away to her room, unlocked her cash box, and took out a thousand gold coins. She also took out a cloak and some other small gifts for her uncle. Then she wrote a letter to him:-

'Greetings, Uncle. Thank you for your letter. I am pleased you sent this messenger who brings news that you are in good health. I have given him the money and a few other items which I hope will be useful.' And she gave the envelope and the bag of coins to the man from the next world' saying, "Take all this to my uncle and tell him to let me know if he is still short of anything, and I will send more."

"Thank you," said the 'man from the next world' who hurried away, amazed that even among the nobility there were people as foolish as his own wife.

As the 'man from the next world' hurried home he passed some fields where he saw an old man hoeing his shamba. "I come from the next world to warn you of great danger," he said.

"What danger?" replied the old man, startled.

"The Sultan is on his way to kill you. He wants to offer you as a sacrifice to the gods so they will watch over his new house. But I have come to save you. Just wear my clothes and I will wear yours, so he won't recognise you," said the 'man from the next world'. The old man immediately did as he was told.

Then the 'man from the next world' said: "Now, climb that coconut tree over there and keep an eye on the road to see if anyone is coming." The old man, who was so frightened he didn't suspect that he was being tricked, clambered up the tree as fast as his old limbs would allow.

Meanwhile the Sultan's wife had told her husband about the 'man from the next world' and had explained what she had done. The Sultan was furious. He shouted: "You foolish woman! Have you taken leave of your senses? Tell me at once which way this man has gone." Then he saddled up his horse, put on his cloak, his turban and his curved broad-bladed dagger and galloped off after the thief.

The old gardener, who was clinging on to the top of the coconut tree, could see the dust clouds rising as the Sultan galloped towards him, and he was terrified. "I can see him

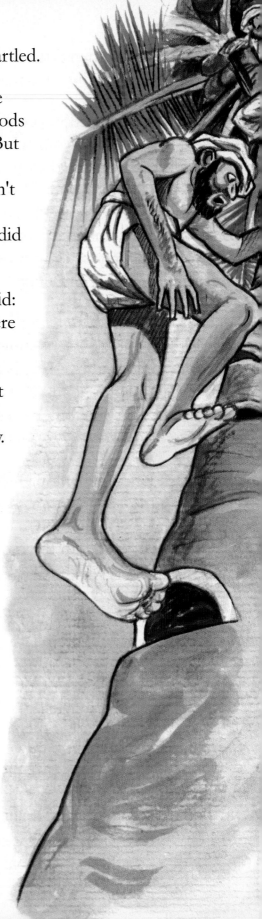

60

coming!" he shouted. But the 'man from the next world' just carried on hoeing.

A few minutes later the Sultan arrived. He asked "Have you seen a man pass this way carrying a bag of money and an envelope?"

The 'man from the next world' answered, "No, but there is a very strange man up that coconut tree over there. He came from the town and he says he is afraid of you. Perhaps he is the man you are looking for."

The Sultan was enraged and wanted to murder the man at the top of the coconut tree. He took off his cloak and his turban and his curved broad-bladed dagger so he had nothing on except a loin cloth and he gave them to the 'man from the next world'. "Hold my horse," he ordered. Then he climbed the coconut tree, shouting to the poor old man at the top: "Now everyone will know what a wicked thief you are!"

The old man at the top of the tree realised that the 'man from the next world' had been right. The Sultan was indeed coming to kill him as a sacrifice for the gods! "What have I done to harm you? Please leave me alone, I am only a poor old gardener," he begged.

But the Sultan just continued to climb the coconut tree, and did not look down. Had he done so he would have seen the 'man from the next world' grasp his bag of money along with the envelope containing the Sultana's reply, don the Sultan's cloak, dagger and turban and gallop off on his horse as fast as he could.

"Where is that man going with your horse and your clothes?" the gardener asked the Sultan. Then the Sultan realised that he had been tricked and that he was just as foolish as his wife and he said to the old gardener, "Please come down and tell me your story."

And when the old man told the Sultan what had happened, and how frightened he had been by the news that he might be offered as a sacrifice to evil spirits the Sultan, instead of being angry, rocked with laughter. Then he told the old man how his wife, too, had been tricked by the 'man from the next world.' "We have all been such fools," they agreed, laughing until their sides ached.

Then the farmer asked the Sultan "What will you tell your wife when you return home?"

And the Sultan replied: "I don't want my wife to know that I am as foolish as she, so I shall tell her that I came upon the 'man from the next world' and that I was so touched by his story that I gave him my horse and all my clothing to take to those in the next world."

"That sounds like a good idea," laughed the old man.

The Sultan returned to his wife and did as he had told the old man, and the 'man from the next world' returned at last to his wife and daughter with his new-found wealth. "I am home!" he shouted, "And I have indeed found not one but three people as foolish as you." And so all was well again between them, but he did warn her: "If our daughter should ever have any more dreams which frighten her, please consult me before you do as the neighbours tell you!"

Why the Cock Crows

Long ago a Cock, a Hen and a Guineafowl lived in the wild, wild woods. But it was a hard life and they spent most of each day hunting for food or being hunted by larger animals.

One winter's day it snowed very heavily in the wild, wild woods. Cock, Hen, and Guineafowl were very cold. Then Cock and Guineafowl said to Hen, "Go into Man's village and ask him to tell you the secret of fire so that we may keep warm."

So Hen set off into the village of Namanyere, where she found man standing by the door of his house.

"*Bwana**," clucked Hen, "I am a creature of the wild, wild woods. Please tell me the secret of your wonderful warm fire so that I may keep myself warm."

"Don't worry about that, my dear Hen," replied Man. "Come along inside and I will keep you warm." But although Man invited Hen inside and shared his food with her, he did not tell her the secret of fire. Hen was quite happy, though, for she no longer needed to work for her food.

She was content to scratch around Man's *shamba** all day and drink and eat from a

* Bwana means 'Sir'

63

wooden bowl like the other animals. She barely noticed that Man was collecting her eggs for himself and because she was warm and cosy she soon forgot all about finding the secret of fire or returning to the wild, wild woods.

After several weeks, when Hen had not returned, Cock became impatient and finally he set off to look for her. When he reached the village he too was offered food and a warm place to sleep and he settled down beside Hen on the cosy straw. But although they had soon raised a large family, Cock remained uneasy about Man and never quite allowed himself to forget about the wild, wild woods. He thought to himself, "Why has Man made us so welcome and yet he has asked for nothing in return?" Over the weeks and months, though, Cock grew used to the easy life of the *shamba*, and soon the wild, wild woods seemed a long way off.

But the goodness of Man was not to last. One day, Man invited his friends and relations to have lunch. Man was at a loss to know what to put in the *kitoweo** dish, until he remembered the fat hen he had tamed and who was now living in the yard.

---

* Shamba means a small holding. It is the plot of land on which country people in Africa traditionally grow their food for the family.

* Kitoweo means 'side dish'. Africans in those days had a mainly vegetarian diet enhanced by meat which was expensive, instead of meat being the main ingredient enhanced by vegetables as we do so kitoweo is the meat 'relish' that goes with the main course.

He went outside and before the surprised Hen realised what was happening he had seized her by the neck. "Not me! Not me!" she squawked. But it was to no avail. Man slaughtered her and served her up for the *kitoweo*.

Cock was terrified. "I knew it was too good to be troooodleooo," he shouted.

At that moment, Guineafowl, who had grown tired of waiting for Cock and Hen to return to the wild, wild wood was coming up the dirt road to the village. When she heard Cock's cry, she screeeched: "Kukuwee! Kukuwee!" which meant, "What's happening? Where is the fire you came to find?"

At this Cock screamed out, "Cockadoodledoo!" Cockadoodledoo !" which meant "Hen is in the fire! We have been deceived! deceived! deceived! Run away! Run away!"

At this Guineafowl ran back to the wild, wild wood as fast as she could. But Cock remained in man's *shamba*, where to this day he warns off wild animals with his loud calls: "Cockadooledoo! Cockadoodledoo!"

A Lazy King is a Happy King

Once, long ago, there lived a King who had three sons, Petro, Joshua and Patriki, each of whom he loved very much. One day when his Councillors assembled in the Council Chamber,   he said to them, "Today is a very important occasion, because I am going to decide who shall be the next King."

"How will you decide between your three sons?" asked an elderly Councillor. "Will you choose the eldest? The strongest? Or perhaps the most handsome?"

"No," said the King, "I will choose the laziest of them all." His Councillors were stunned.

"But, Your Majesty, why would you want to choose the laziest? Surely that is not a Kingly virtue?" they asked.

"I sit here all day and I do nothing, and I know that if I were not a lazy man I would go mad," explained the King. "A lazy King is a happy King. Now come over to this baobab tree and let my sons be brought to me immediately."

66

A few moments later the three young men came galloping towards the King. Each dismounted and came to stand before their father. "My sons," said the King, "I have a very important announcement to make. I am going to decide who will be the next King."

"I am the oldest," said Petro.

"I am the strongest," said Joshua.

"I am the most handsome," said Patriki.

"You don't need to be old, or strong, or handsome to be King," said their father. "You need to be very very lazy because a lazy King is a happy King. And whoever is the laziest of you all will inherit my Kingdom."

So the three young men mounted their horses and galloped away, far up the dusty track which led from their father's palace to their own quarters, each planning how he would prove he was lazier than his brothers.

Some weeks later the eldest son, Petro, limped slowly up the dusty track to the gates of his father's palace. "Look at my legs!" he shouted to his father. "Do you wonder why they are so red and sore?"

"What have you done?" asked his father, horrified at the burns which covered them.

"When I was sitting by the fire and a log fell out onto my legs I was too lazy to move it, so you can see how badly they have been burned."

"That is indeed lazy," said the King and he summoned a herbalist to heal the wounds.

The next day Joshua arrived at the palace gates "I have thought of a way to prove how lazy I am," he told his father.

"How's that?" asked the King. "Well, if you first give

me a knife and then tie a rope around my ankle and hang me from that baobab tree I will be too lazy to cut myself free," said Joshua.

"So the King ordered that Joshua be given a knife and then hung by the feet from the baobab tree, and he was still hanging there several hours later when his third son Patriki arrived.

"Wait till you hear how lazy I have been," said Patriki proudly. "Last night I was lying in my bed when smoke started to rise from a fire which had started in the kitchen below. My eyes were streaming and I was choking to death, but I continued to lie there without moving until my two brothers dragged me from my bed and out of the house."

"Aha!" said the King. "Now we know who is really the laziest. You did not even get up to save your own life but your brothers did it for you. You shall indeed be the next king."

Mpenzi and the Golden Bird

Once upon a time in Africa there lived a King and Queen who had two sons, Prince Yusufu and Prince Chepe. Some years later the Queen died. The poor King was heartbroken but the two princes did nothing to comfort their father for they had grown up to be spoilt and selfish men. They ordered the King around all day and never lifted so much as a finger to do anything for themselves. Indeed, they saw no reason to do anything for they imagined that they would one day inherit their father's kingdom and be rich for ever. And so the two princes grew fatter and lazier and the poor King grew lonelier with each passing day.

Some years later the King met a lovely young woman with whom he fell in love and married. The new Queen gave birth to a son, whom they named *Mpenzi* - 'special one'.

Yusufu and Chepe became very jealous of *Mpenzi* because they could see that he was their father's favourite.

One day, when *Mpenzi* was about six years old, he was walking with his father in the palace gardens when he heard a wonderful singing. He looked up and caught sight of a beautiful bird, high in the branches of a baobab tree. "Look, father," said *Mpenzi*, pointing to the bird preening its feathers on the top branch.

When the King looked up, he was amazed to
see a bird with feathers of gold,
and feet the colour of pearls.
"It is the most perfect thing
I have ever seen," he said. But
as he drew nearer, the bird flew
away, and although the boy and his
father searched high and low for it
every day, they didn't see it again.

71

Shortly afterwards, the King, who was by now very old, became ill. And although they had barely visited him since his second marriage, Yusufu and Chepe now rushed to their father's bedside, pretending to be concerned.

"What is it you want?" the King asked them.

"We want to know which of us will inherit your throne," they said.

The King told them about the beautiful bird he had seen in the palace garden, and then he said: "Whoever brings the golden bird back to live in my garden will inherit my kingdom."

Then the King gave Yusufu and Chepe each one hundred servants and one hundred gold coins to help them in their search and bid them farewell. Meanwhile, *Mpenzi*, who had overheard the conversation,

crept softly into the room and sat on the end
of his father's bed.

"I will bring the bird to you," he said.

"You are too young to think or do such things,"
said the King. But *Mpenzi* begged and pleaded
until finally the King agreed to allow him to
join his brothers on the safari. He gave him
a hundred servants and a hundred gold coins
like his brothers, and told Yusufu and Chepe to
take good care of him.

The three sons bid their father good-bye. But as soon as they were out of his sight, Yusufu and Chepe seized *Mpenzi* and held a knife to his throat. "Now you will never inherit what is rightfully ours," they said.

"Please don't kill me," pleaded their little brother. "Take these servants and this money, but spare my life."

"He will never catch the bird anyway," agreed the brothers, so they took the servants and money and left *Mpenzi* alone in the forest where they were sure he would soon be eaten by wild animals.

Then Yusufu and Chepe, who could not think of any other plan, made a trap for the bird and returned to their homes where they set their servants to work on the land while they grew fat and lazy.

Meanwhile, *Mpenzi* walked deeper and deeper into the bush until he found a cave in which to hide. He was just drifting off to sleep when he heard a huge growl. He had awoken an enormous bear that had been asleep at the back of the cave and was now very angry at being disturbed. The bear leapt at *Mpenzi*, who only just managed to escape.

Mpenzi ran as fast as he could through the bush until he came to a desert which stretched as far as the eye could see.

In the middle of the desert stood a solitary tree. Exhausted, *Mpenzi* leaned back against it and closed his eyes.

It wasn't until he heard a huge roar from above him that he realised to his horror that he had been leaning not against a tree trunk but the legs of a giant creature. "Fee! Fi! Fo! Foy! I smell the blood of a little boy!" the giant shouted. Poor *Mpenzi* was terrified.

He only just managed to reply, in a small, trembling voice, "I am lost. Please do not eat me."

"Ha!" replied the giant, whose name was *Zimwi*. "Don't flatter yourself! You would not be enough for a snack! Still, you've just enough blood for me to gargle with, and your bones would make good toothpicks if I removed and ate all the meat on you first."

The terrified boy could only whisper, "Please spare me!"

"Tell me why you are here," demanded *Zimwi*. *Mpenzi* told him all about his sick father's wish for the golden bird and how his brothers had taken his money and servants and left him to die.

"Tell me where these wicked brothers are and I shall eat them for my lunch," roared *Zimwi*. But *Mpenzi* could not bear to think of his father's grief if he discovered his two elder sons were dead.

Instead he said, "I was chased by a huge bear on my way. He was in the cave over there."

"Stay here," ordered Zimwi, leaving the terrified boy trembling while he dashed into the forest to catch the bear. After a short while, Zimwi returned patting his vast stomach. "That's much better," he said. "Now, is there anything I can do for you in return?"

"Please help me to find the golden bird," replied *Mpenzi*. "My father will not live for much longer and he wants so much to see it again. It might even make him feel well again."

"Well," said *Zimwi* thoughtfully, "As it happens I know where those birds live. Come on, I'll show you." They travelled for six days until they came within sight of a great golden palace.

"In the courtyard of that great golden palace you will find a great golden tree," said *Zimwi*. "In the great golden tree you will find the great golden birds. But first you will have to creep past the great golden ogre, and he is even bigger than I am and even hungrier. If he sees you he will probably devour you with one lick of his lips."

Mpenzi was terrified, but he crept up to the gates and slid underneath. He could see no sign of the great golden ogre, but he could see the tree and the beautiful birds in the courtyard beyond and he ran quickly to the foot of the tree and started to climb up to their nest. He was just reaching out to touch one of the birds when he heard the terrible roar of the great golden ogre. It was like thunder and screams all rolled into one and when *Mpenzi* saw him he was petrified.

The great golden ogre was the size of a massive tower block and he was golden from head to foot, with long greasy strands of golden hair

hanging down as far as his waist and a golden beard like a shiny forest covering most of his face. He smelt as if he hadn't had a bath for years, and large creatures with long legs were climbing in and out of his hair.

"What are you doing? Do you dare to steal my magical birds?" he roared, picking *Mpenzi* up and almost squashing him to death between his thumb and forefinger.

At first *Mpenzi* could not answer; his voice had deserted him. Then he whispered, "I don't think you should eat me."

"Give me one good reason why not!" said the ogre, staring hard at *Mpenzi*. He had the most enormous bulging eyes *Mpenzi* had ever seen. Each was the size of a hill, with a deep dark lake in the middle.

"*Zimwi* sent me," *Mpenzi* whispered.

"*Zimwi*, eh?" said the ogre, "Well, if *Zimwi* hasn't eaten you, there must be something very nasty about you. But why were you trying to catch my golden birds?"

"My father is very ill and his only wish is to see your beautiful golden birds once again before he dies."

"Ah," said the ogre, his mouth opening like a huge black cave to reveal teeth like jagged rocks.

He put *Mpenzi* gently down in the palm of his huge left hand while he thoughtfully scratched his beard with the fingers of his right hand, sending the animals scurrying madly about.

Then he said slowly, "If you bring me the Great Sword of Thunder I will let you have a pair of my magical birds to take to your father."

"Where will I find it?" asked *Mpenzi*.

"It is in the house of the Great Dragon of Thunder," replied the ogre. "*Zimwi* knows where he lives. Ask him to show you."

"Very well," replied *Mpenzi*. "I will bring it to you." The great golden ogre put him back onto the ground outside the palace gates and *Mpenzi* ran as fast as his legs would carry him back to Zimwi, who was amazed to see him still alive.

"The great golden ogre says I must bring him the Great Sword of Thunder if I am to have his golden birds," he told *Zimwi* when he reached him.

"The Great Sword of Thunder belongs to the Great Dragon of Thunder who lives across the sea on the Island of Storm," said *Zimwi*. "But no one has ever dared to go there for he is so big and evil that he makes the great golden ogre look like a harmless gnome."

"I am not afraid," said the brave *Mpenzi*.

"Very well," replied *Zimwi*, "I will make a huge canoe to carry us both there." Then he tore

up some giant trees and made a big canoe and they sailed across the sea to the Island of Storm.

Mpenzi crept into the vast palace of the Great Dragon of Thunder and looked around him. High on the wall above the Dragon's throne he saw the Sword of Thunder shining brightly. *Mpenzi* started to climb slowly towards it. He was just stretching out his hand to take the sword when all at once a terrible voice thundered, "Who goes there?"

Mpenzi shut his eyes tightly for he did not even dare to look at the Great Dragon of Thunder.

Thinking quickly *Mpenzi* said, "I have come to grant you a wish. If you will tell me what you would like most of all, I will bring it to you in exchange for this sword."

The Dragon was quite taken aback. He was not used to people trying to bargain with him. He was so big and so evil and so ugly that most people just ran away at the sight of him. Nevertheless he was just about to stamp on the little boy when he stopped and thought for a moment.

"There is something I would like," he said. "I am very lonely here. I would like two evil henchmen to live with me and keep me company and guard the palace from intruders like you."

"Very well," replied *Mpenzi*. "I will bring them to you if you will give me the Great Sword of Thunder."

The Dragon agreed and *Mpenzi* left more quickly than he had arrived. To Zimwi's great surprise, *Mpenzi* emerged unharmed. "What happened?" he asked curiously.

When *Mpenzi* told him what he had agreed with the Dragon, Zimwi laughed so loudly that the trees around them shook. "I think we know the perfect pair of evil henchmen," he said.

Mpenzi knew at once that he meant Yusufu and Chepe. "But how will you catch them?" he asked.

"We will have to be very clever," said Zimwi. "Tomorrow you must go to your brothers and convince them that you have a secret potion which will grant them everlasting life. But be sure to tell them that this wonderful medicine is only successful when it is taken at sea."

And so in the morning they set sail just as the
sun was rising. When they reached land, *Mpenzi*
went to the town where his brothers lived.
They were also very surprised to see him still
alive, but intrigued when he told them of his
discovery.

They quickly agreed to come with him to the
canoe and try some of his amazing potion.
Once the canoe had set sail, *Zimwi* showed
himself. The two brothers were terrified. "You
are evil men," said Zimwi. "You left your little
brother all alone in the forest, hoping that he
would die."

"Please don't hurt us," begged Yusufu and Chepe.

When they reached the Island of Thunder
Zimwi tucked the brothers under one arm and
Mpenzi safely under the other and marched up
to the palace gates, calling: "Oh! Great Dragon
of Thunder. We have brought you two evil
henchmen for company." The Great Dragon of
Thunder was delighted to see them.

"Take the sword," he said to *Mpenzi*.

Then *Zimwi* and *Mpenzi* went on their way with
the Sword of Thunder, leaving Yusufu and
Chepe to keep the dragon company When they
reached the Great Golden Palace *Mpenzi* strode
proudly in. "I have brought you the Great
Sword of Thunder," he called to the ogre. The
ogre beamed the most huge and golden smile
which lit up the whole of the castle. Then he
took the sword and examined it carefully.

"You are a very brave and clever boy," he said to *Mpenzi*. "Here is a pair of golden birds. They will stay with you in the palace gardens forever and make your father feel well again."

Mpenzi carefully carried the birds, one on each hand, back to Zimwi.

"Go back to your father," said *Zimwi*. Then he handed him a feather. "Take this feather with you. It will keep you safe and if ever you need me, just put it in the fire and I will appear."

When *Mpenzi* returned to his father's palace there was great rejoicing. His father took the golden birds, and at once he was made well again. When *Mpenzi* told him the story of how he had been helped by *Zimwi* and had bargained with the ogre and the dragon he was amazed.

"You have proved yourself to be the bravest and best of my sons," he said. "One day you will be a very fine King."

So *Mpenzi* worked hard to learn his father's kingly ways and many years later when his father was very old he died peacefully in his sleep and *Mpenzi* was crowned king.

Mpenzi always kept the feather which *Zimwi* had given him to keep him safe. There were times in his life when he did call his friend *Zimwi* for help and I'll tell you about those another day...

The Sheep who Prayed

Once upon a time there lived a poor man and his wife whose only possessions were a sheep and a cockerel. One day they heard that a distant cousin was to visit them.

"What shall we eat?" asked the poor woman in despair. "We have eaten everything except our sheep and our cockerel."

"It seems a shame to kill either of them," said her husband.

The couple discussed the matter for several days before finally deciding to kill the sheep. The sheep was terrified.

All night he prayed to God to save him. "Baa! Baa!" he called softly, which meant, "Please don't let me die. I will provide wool for the poor man and his wife to make into clothes to keep them warm." He said this over and over again, all night long, but quietly so as not to wake the couple up and thereby hasten his death.

But the cockerel, who was a thoughtless bird, crowed all night, "Cockadoodledoo! Cockadoodledoo!" which meant, "Kill the sheep! Let's kill the sheep!"

84

When dawn broke, the poor man and his wife got out of bed but they had not slept because of the terrible noise the cockerel had made all night.

"I can't stand another night like that," said the poor man. "Let's kill the noisy cockerel instead of the sheep. After all, our visitor is only here for one meal and I'm sure there will be enough to go round."

And so the sheep's prayer was answered but the noisy cockerel was roasted for lunch.

The Three Clever Children

There was once a man who had three clever children, but he was very sick and knew that he would soon die. He had only a little money to leave to his family, but he was determined that they should all become wealthy after he died.

So he told each of his children in turn that after his death they would inherit nothing until they had first made some money out of the local Sultan, who was very rich.

After their father had died, the three children set off to carry out his wishes. On the way, the Eldest saw a footprint in the sand.

"This is the footprint of a camel," he said.

The Second said, "It must have been carrying a heavy weight."

And the Third exclaimed, "It must have passed by at least an hour ago!"

Further along the way they met a man.

"Did you pass my animal?" he asked.

"Was it a camel?" asked the Eldest.

"Yes," replied the man.

"Was it carrying a heavy load?" asked the Second.

"Yes," replied the man.

"Did it pass by about an hour ago?" asked the Third.

"Yes. How did you know all this?" asked the man. But the three children just smiled and walked on.

A little further on they came across some more footprints.

"Those are human footprints," said the Eldest child.

"They were made by a woman," said the Second. "Here is her bracelet. She must have been carrying a child on her back, who played with it and then dropped it," said the Third.

Shortly afterwards they met another man.

"I say, gentlemen, have you by any chance seen anyone pass this way ?" he asked.

The Eldest asked, "Was it a lady?"

"Yes," replied the man.

"Did she have a gold bracelet like this," asked the Second.

"Yes," replied the man, snatching it from him.

"Was she carrying a child on her back?" asked the Third.

"Yes," replied the man.

"Where is she?" But the three just smiled and walked on.

When the three clever children arrived at the Sultan's house, he made them very welcome and invited them to feast with him and his family. He ordered that a goat should be killed in their honour and served with locally-grown rice.

When everyone had begun to eat, the Eldest child said, "This rice tastes as if it has been grown in a graveyard."

The Second said, "This goat does not taste as if it was fed with its mother's milk."

And the Third said, "You are not really the true Sultan are you?"

The Sultan was furious at their impudence. "Whatever are you talking about?" he shouted. "I have welcomed you into my home and offered you food and all you do is insult me."

But the three clever children replied, "We have only spoken the truth."

"Why did you say the rice I gave you was grown in a graveyard?" he asked the Eldest, who replied:

"Only rice that is grown in a graveyard is so well grown. Surely it is forbidden to grow crops in that way isn't it?" The Sultan could not believe his ears.

"It is," he admitted. "Why did you say that the goat was not fed on its mother's milk?" he asked the Second.

"I could taste that the goat had been fed on the milk of a donkey, not its true mother," he replied.

"Why did you say I was not the true Sultan?" he asked the Third.

"I can tell by your eyes that you are the son of another," he replied.

The Sultan was enraged. He called for his Advisor and asked where the rice had come from.

He replied, "It was grown in a graveyard."

"How was the goat fed?" asked the Sultan.

"Its mother died when it was very young and it was suckled by a donkey," replied the Advisor.

Then the Sultan called in his mother and asked her, "Am I the Sultan, and son of my dead father the Sultan?"

But his mother replied, "Indeed you are not his son, but the son of my first husband."

The Sultan was speechless with amazement. But before he had time to think of anything to say,

89

the man who had lost his camel arrived. When he saw the children, he immediately accused them of stealing it.

"Tell me the truth," ordered the Sultan. "Did you steal this man's camel?"

"No, we have never even seen it," replied the children. But the camel's owner asked, "How else could you tell me so much about it when I met you on the road?"

The Eldest replied, "I knew that it was a camel because of the shape of its footprints in the sand."

The Second replied, "I knew it was carrying a heavy load because its footmarks were deep."

Then the Third said, "I knew that it had passed by an hour before because its footprints were sand-blown."

The Sultan said "It's obvious these children are telling the truth. They did not steal your camel. Case dismissed."

Then the man who had lost his wife appeared before the Sultan.

"These children have kidnapped my wife," he said.

"Did you kidnap this man's wife?" asked the Sultan. "No, we did not even see her," answered the three children.

"How then could you tell me so much about her when I met you on the road?" asked the man.

The Eldest replied, "I recognised the footprints as that of a person."

"I knew that she was a woman because they were the shape of women's feet," said the Second.

"I knew that she had a child on her back because she would not have left her bracelet behind without a reason. She must have given it to the child to play with and he must have dropped it without his mother knowing," said the third.

And the Sultan said, "It is obvious that these children did not kidnap your wife. Case dismissed."

"These are truly amazing children," thought the Sultan to himself. But he felt shamed by their revelation that he was not the true son of the dead Sultan, and he decided to get rid of them. First he showered them with money and gifts. Then he gave them each a red cloak and bid them a safe journey home. He gave each of his own children a black cloak and bid them accompany them.

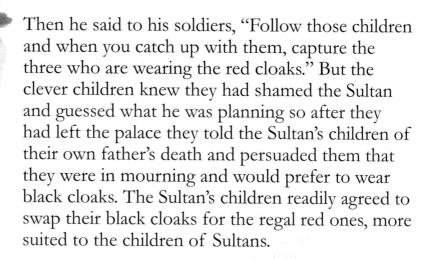

Then he said to his soldiers, "Follow those children and when you catch up with them, capture the three who are wearing the red cloaks." But the clever children knew they had shamed the Sultan and guessed what he was planning so after they had left the palace they told the Sultan's children of their own father's death and persuaded them that they were in mourning and would prefer to wear black cloaks. The Sultan's children readily agreed to swap their black cloaks for the regal red ones, more suited to the children of Sultans.

When the soldiers caught up with them they captured the Sultan's children instead of the three clever children, who returned home to their mother with their new-found wealth, fulfilling their father's wishes, and they lived happily ever after.

How the Hyena got his Coat

One day Old Lion was out hunting when he came
upon a herd of buffalo. After a mighty battle he
brought one down and killed it. But the fierce struggle
had left him exhausted and his paw was wounded.

Old Lion was so tired that he lay panting in a heap by the door of a
cave. Just then along came Wild Cat. "What is wrong with your paw?"
he asked the lion. Old Lion explained what had happened. Then he
asked Wild Cat to cook the buffalo and bring him the best parts of it -
the head, heart, liver and kidneys.

But Wild Cat, too, was hungry. He cooked the meat, but kept the best
bits for himself, bringing back only the gristly and fatty parts for Old
Lion. When Old Lion asked what had happened, Wild Cat lied and said
that the best bits had burned in the fire while the meat was cooking. Old
Lion knew that Wild Cat was lying but he kept quiet because, although in
normal circumstances he could have killed the cat with one swipe of his
mighty paw, he was still wounded and needed Wild Cat's help.

But some days later, when his paw was a bit better, Old Lion grabbed
the Wild Cat and roared at him, "I know you lied to me about the
meat, so unless you stay here and become my slave I will kill you."

Wild Cat was so scared that he agreed to stay with Old Lion and for many months he fetched his food, and his water, and did whatever else Old Lion ordered him to do. After a time, he grew fond of Old Lion and the two became the best of friends.

Not long after that, Hyena came to see Old Lion. Old Lion was pleased to see him, and sent Wild Cat to fetch food for their guest. Wild Cat, who knew that hyenas like bones best, fetched a large pile which Hyena ate hungrily.

But Hyena was jealous of Wild Cat's friendship with Old Lion. "What cunning plan can I devise to eat his bones?" he said to himself. He went away to think about it and after a few days he came back to see Old Lion.

"How are you?" asked Hyena.

"Oh, I'm a bit better, but I'm still lame," replied Old Lion.

"Hasn't Wild Cat given you any special treatment?" asked Hyena.

"What treatment?" asked Old Lion.

"Do you mean to say you don't know that Wild Cat is a famous healer?" asked Hyena.

Old Lion was very surprised and a bit angry at this news so when Wild Cat brought in a tray of food he grabbed him by his tail, and roared, "Why haven't you made me better? Hyena says you have known all along how to cure me, so why am I still lame? I'm going to kill you if you don't make me better."

At first Wild Cat was very confused. Then, as the hyena began to laugh his wicked laugh, he realised how cunning he had been. But he didn't panic, he just stayed silent. "Why are you so quiet?" roared Old Lion. "Hurry up and answer me before I silence you for ever."

"I am quiet, sir, because the cure for your lameness isn't easy to find," replied Wild Cat carefully.

"Just tell me - before I finish you off," said Old Lion.

"Well," said Wild Cat carefully, "My father once told me that the only medicine for a wound like yours is the skin from the back of a hyena. If you cover your wound with it you will be better in no time."

At this Hyena started to slink away, but Old Lion was too quick for him and he leapt upon his back. Hyena screamed out, "Lion, please stop, he's making it all up..." But Old Lion held on until he had taken a long strip of skin from his back. Then Hyena rushed home screaming with pain, because of the skin torn from his back. Meanwhile Wild Cat bound the skin tightly round the wound on Old Lion's paw. In a few days the lion, whose paw had already been healing, was completely better and he knew that 'Doctor' Wild Cat must have spoken the truth. Wild Cat stayed with Old Lion, and Old Lion thought of him even more as a friend, and guarded him well.

But the hyena suffered terribly, so that even today if you look at his back you will see a peculiar patch where long hairs have grown over the scar.

How the Turtle Got His Shell

Long ago, in the days before Turtle had a shell, the creatures of the sea each had their place in the circle of life. Big fish ate smaller fish and they in turn ate those who were smaller still. But they took only what they needed to survive and there was always plenty of food for everyone.

Then along came Man. At first, he fished only for what he needed, using his bare hands or sharp sticks. Then he started to hunt for a few extra fish so he could exchange them for other things he needed. But as time went on his methods became more clever as he started to use traps, hooks and nets.

Whale, who was King of the sea creatures, was worried that as the years passed Man might discover even more terrible ways of harvesting the fruits of the sea. So he decided to call a meeting of all the sea creatures to discuss how they might best protect themselves from being harmed by Man.

All the creatures of the sea gathered at Whale's fine palace one afternoon. All, that is, except Turtle. "Where is Turtle?" asked Whale. "Does he think he is so important that he doesn't need to listen to what I am going to say about Man and the terrible things he is planning to do to us?"

"I will send my son to fetch him," said Crab. So Little Crab hurried in his sideways-sort-of-way as quickly as he could to Turtle's home under the large flat rock. When he arrived he found Turtle, who in those days had no shell, on his hands and knees mumbling some words which Little Crab couldn't understand.

"What are you doing?" asked Little Crab.

"Don't you know that Whale has commanded us all to a meeting at his palace? Why are you still at home?"

"Is Almighty God there?" asked Turtle.

Little Crab was taken aback. "No, there was no one of that name. Who is Almighty God?" he asked.

"I've never heard of him. Where does he live and what does he look like?"

"I know only that he will take care of me," replied Turtle.

Little Crab could see that he was getting nowhere in his efforts to persuade Turtle to come to the meeting with him so he hurried back in his sideways-sort-of-way to tell Whale what had happened. "What nonsense!" shouted Whale when Little Crab told him about Turtle. "How dare Turtle disobey my orders! He must be punished at once for such stupidity!"

Little Crab feared for Turtle's life and he took a short cut ahead of the other creatures back to Turtle's home under the large flat rock. "Hide, Turtle!" he warned him. "Whale and all the other sea creatures are coming to your house and they are very angry with you."

"Is Almighty God with them?" asked Turtle.

"Please, Turtle, stop talking about this Almighty God. He won't be able to help you now," pleaded Little Crab.

"Don't worry," said Turtle. "I know He will look after me."

Little Crab shook his head in despair. He hurried back to the other animals and pretended to join them in case they became angry with him too.

But when the animals arrived at Turtle's house they could not see him anywhere. Little Crab waited until they had given up hunting and then he called softly, "Turtle! It is I, your friend, Little Crab. Where are you hiding?"

"Here!" came a muffled reply.

It took Crab several minutes to work out where the voice was coming from. Then he realised that Turtle was hiding under a large shell which was almost the same colour as the bottom of the sea. "You are well-hidden," said Crab. "How did you manage to find such a convenient shell to hide in?"

"Almighty God gave it to me," said Turtle. "From now on, all turtles will have a special shell to protect them from Man and from other animals." Crab was astonished. He tugged and pulled on Turtle's shell. But it stayed in place no matter what.

Then he called to the other animals. "Come and see what Turtle's Almighty God has done for him."

One by one the other animals came to see Turtle's shell and they forgot their anger in their astonishment at what had happened.

"How did you get your shell?" they asked.

"Almighty God gave it to me. If you have faith in Him he will look after you," explained Turtle.

And although the sea creatures did not find a way to avoid man's exploitation of the sea, they did learn about Almighty God that day and some say that he is now their only hope of survival.

The Sultan and his Clever Daughter

There was once a Sultan who had only one child, a daughter whom he loved very much. At school she was always top of the class, and he was proud of her great intelligence. At the same school was a poor boy, Sefu, with whom the Sultan's daughter fell in love. And despite a long line of rich suitors, the Sultan's daughter wanted only Sefu, whom she claimed was cleverer than the rest of them put together.

The Sultan (who was not as clever as his daughter) was confused because he couldn't understand why she would want to marry someone so poor. But his daughter insisted, saying: "I am in love with him and I promise you he is really very clever."

When the Sultan saw that his daughter had made up her mind to marry the poor scholar, he decided to go along with it, but to put the young man's intelligence to the test. The Sultan summoned Sefu and said, "I am going to visit some people and I would like you to come with me."

Along the way the Sultan and Sefu came to some tall rice plants which had ripened and had been tied up with string.

And the boy asked the Sultan "What is this?"

"Don't you know? It's rice, of course," replied the Sultan.

"And what is it tied up with?" asked the boy.

"String," replied the Sultan, adding, "I'm surprised you didn't know that."

By and by, a little further along the way they came upon a crowd of men who were employed as bird scarers. They were running about in all directions, waving their arms and shouting *"Hao! Hao! Hao!"* And as the Sultan and Sefu passed they continued to shout *"Hao! Hao! Hao!"* "What are those people doing?" asked Sefu.

"Are you totally stupid?" asked the Sultan.

"Can't you see that they are scaring away the birds?"

By and by, a little further along the way, they came upon water holes, some on the surface, and some deep wells in the ground. In some of the places people were bathing and in others they were drawing water to drink. "What are these people doing?" asked Sefu.

By now the Sultan was in despair. This young man was turning out to be even more of an idiot than he could have imagined. "Can't you see?" he asked incredulously, "Some of them are bathing in the water and some of them are drawing water to drink."

"Ah," replied Sefu thoughtfully. And so they went on their way until they reached their destination where they were offered a cup of coffee which they gratefully accepted, for it had been a long dusty walk.

The coffee was passed to Sefu who, instead of passing it on to the Sultan to drink first, sipped it himself. And the Sultan, who was not accustomed to such bad manners in his presence, was horrified. "Not only is this youth an idiot, but he clearly has no manners either," he thought to himself.

On the way home, the Sultan could barely bring himself to speak to Sefu, because he was so angry. When they reached the Sultan's house his daughter came running out to greet them.

"How did you get on with your future son-in-law?" she asked her father.

"I don't want to hear another word about this mannerless idiot," replied her father, dismissing Sefu who went sadly away.

When he had calmed down, his daughter asked: "What has made you so angry with Sefu?"

"First of all we came upon some rice tied up with twine and Sefu asked what it was," began the Sultan.

"Do you know why he asked?" his daughter asked him.

"It is because sometimes young trees grow like rice but they can fall and ruin a rice crop."

"Yes, I suppose that is

true," admitted the Sultan. "But he's still an idiot and I'll tell you why: when we were passing through a field full of bird scarers he asked what they were doing."

But his daughter said, "Father, why are you so surprised about that? The bird scarers were not showing the Sultan and his future son-in-law respect by falling silent as you passed. Instead they treated you as if you were birds."

"Yes, I suppose that is true," admitted the Sultan. "But he's still an idiot and I'll tell you why." Then he told her about how Sefu had asked what the people were doing at the water holes and how he had helped himself first to the coffee.

And his daughter answered, "Surely that is quite clear! He was worried that the coffee had been made with the water in which people had been bathing and not with the drinking water and so he knew he must taste it first to safeguard you in case it was poisoned."

"Yes, I suppose that is true," said the Sultan, and indeed when he thought about it, he realised how very quick thinking his future son-in-law was and he had to admit that the couple were well suited in terms of their intelligence, which they were, weren't they?

The Tale of the Three Idiots

Once upon a time a man was walking along when he passed three men sitting by the side of the road passing the time of day. "Good morning, Idiot," he said and they all replied, "Greetings to you, too."

Now most people would feel offended if they had just been addressed as 'Idiot' by a total stranger, but not so these three. They immediately started arguing about who the passer by had been addressing.

The first said, "He was obviously talking to me!"

The second said "No, I am the Idiot."

The third said, "My wife always calls me Idiot, so I'm sure he must be one of her friends."

After they had argued like this for a while, one of them (who was possibly a little less of an Idiot than the others) suggested that they should catch up with the stranger and ask him whom he was addressing when he said, "Good morning Idiot."

They ran as fast as they could and when they caught up with the stranger the first Idiot asked, "Were you calling me 'Idiot'? I am sure you must have been for I am indeed stupid and I'll tell you why:

"Yesterday I went to the market and bought some meat for my wife to cook. While it was cooking I took two pieces out of the pan and put them in my mouth while my wife wasn't looking, but they were boiling hot and when my wife saw me hopping around with my mouth burning she said, 'Spit it out, quick!' but by then it had badly burnt my mouth and I haven't been able to eat a thing since. Don't you think I am a complete Idiot now?" and the stranger as well as his companions all agreed that he was.

Then the second man said, "But I too am an Idiot. vYesterday I went to the market and bought meat, rice, a coconut and other ingredients for making a curry, which I gave to my wife to cook. There is a rule in my village that at ten o'clock in the evening everyone must be at home. It is the Sultan's orders that anyone found with doors open later gets locked up for the night and executed in the morning.

By the time our food was ready it was nearly ten o'clock and my wife told me to close the door before we sat down to eat.

But I said, "What do you think I am? Your slave? You close the door!" and so we quarrelled about who should close the door, while the food sat on the table uneaten. Meanwhile a dog came into the house and ate the curry, but still we argued.

Finally, at eleven o'clock a policeman arrived and asked us why we had not obeyed the Sultan's orders but we just continued to argue so he locked us up for the night to await execution. We begged and pleaded and eventually we were allowed home but can you imagine anyone behaving in a more idiotic way than that?" The stranger and his companions all agreed that he certainly was an Idiot too.

Then it was the turn of the third man: "I am an even bigger idiot of all my companions," he said, "Last week I had a toothache and I went to visit a dentist. I said to him, 'My tooth hurts. Do you know how to extract it?' The dentist assured me he did, and he said it would cost fifty pence. I didn't have a fifty pence piece but I did have a ten pound note so I asked him to take out twenty teeth instead! As you can see I've only got a few left now! Don't you think I am the biggest Idiot of all?" The stranger and his companions agreed that he was certainly a strong contender for the title.

The stranger, who by now felt he knew the three quite well, replied "I always say, 'If the cap fits, wear it'" whereupon he handed them three caps marked 'Idiot' which they all wore proudly from that day onwards.

The Sultan's Son and the Rich Man's Daughter

Once upon a time a Sultan and a rich man became friends. The Sultan had a son and the rich man had a daughter and it was decided that they should be married. It was a huge wedding, with guests from every direction, near and far. The dancing and feasting lasted for a whole week. And everyone, even the servants, were allowed to join in the celebrations. It was almost impossible to speak or hear for the noise of merriment!

For seven days they feasted and on the seventh day the couple departed on their honeymoon, which lasted for seven months, at the end of which the Sultan ordered his servants to dig the foundations for a wonderful new house for the newly- weds.

But when the Sultan's son took his new bride to see the house which was being built he did a very strange thing. He told her to come with him and take a closer look and while they were there, he suddenly grasped her by the shoulders and pushed her into a deep pit dug for the foundations.

And when she begged and pleaded for him to get her out, he told her that he had become bored with her and he was leaving to find a new wife in Muscat.

But his wife, who had magic powers, just said calmly, "Fine. I'm going to give birth to your three children while you are away."

The Sultan's son laughed loud and long and mocked his wife, saying, "I don't know how you think you are going to bear my three children when you are stuck down in that pit and I am leaving the country tomorrow."

The Sultan's son ordered three bags of millet, one of maize and a container of water to be lowered into the pit. Then he packed up for his trip and left. "I'll go and find a prettier wife now," he said unkindly, as he left her at the bottom of the pit. Shortly after he had left, some large long-tailed rats came to the pit.

"Why are you in this pit?" they asked.

"I married the Sultan's son seven months ago, but he no longer loves me," she said sadly. "He has left me in this pit and gone to find a new and prettier wife. I think he wants me to die."

The large long-tailed rats said, "How dreadful!" and they discussed the problem between themselves for a few minutes. Then they did a wonderful thing! They dug a hole from the pit all the way to her mother's bedroom.

Well, you can imagine her mother's surprise when her daughter crawled up underneath her bed in the middle of the night.

"How did you get in here when all the doors and windows are shut?" she asked her. Then her daughter broke down sobbing, and told her mother all that had happened since she had returned from her honeymoon. "That's terrible!" said her mother. "What are you going to do?"

"I am going to sail after him and use my magic powers to get even with him," replied her daughter. The next day she set sail, with her own crew of women, and they performed their magic which enabled her to reach Muscat disguised as a prettier woman before her husband's ship.

When she arrived there she went to see the Sultan of Muscat. "Behind me comes a man with whom I have had a disagreement", she said. "When he arrives he will be looking for a wife and I want you to adopt me as your daughter and offer me to him as his wife. I promise to pay you well for this." And the Sultan agreed to do as she had asked.

As soon as the Sultan's son reached Muscat, he dropped anchor and fired off his cannons. Three days later he went to pay his respects to the Sultan and to seek his daughter's hand in marriage. The Sultan agreed and so it was arranged. The young man stayed for exactly a year during which time the girl bore him a daughter. The young man gave the child gold trinkets, and never did he realise that his new wife was the same one that he had thrown in the pit.

But by the end of the year the Sultan's son had tired of his 'new' wife and set off on another trip to the land of Guava in Arabia. "We'll see about that," thought his wife and she boarded her own ship with her daughter and her servants and using her magic powers she managed to reach Guava first, disguised once again.

Then she went to see the Sultan of Guava. And when she reached the Sultan she said, "Behind me comes a man with whom I have had a disagreement. When he arrives he will be looking for a wife and I want you to adopt me as your daughter and offer me to him as a wife. I promise to pay you well for this." And the Sultan agreed to do as she had asked.

Once more the pair settled down together for exactly a year, while the girl's servants secretly looked after their daughter and this time the rich man's daughter bore a son. Her husband bestowed many special gifts upon him, before he tired of his 'new' wife and set off, this time to the Land of the Lime Tree. "We'll see about that," thought the rich man's daughter and once again she set sail in her own ship and used her

magic powers to disguise herself and arrive before him, leaving her children on the ship with her servants.

This time she went to see the Sultan of The Land of The Lime Tree. And when she reached the Sultan she said, "Behind me comes a man with whom I have had a disagreement. When he arrives he will be looking for a wife and I want you to adopt me as your daughter and offer me to him as a wife. I promise to pay you well for this." And the Sultan agreed to do as she had asked.

The young man again married her and this time she bore him another daughter. Again he gave presents to the child and after exactly a year he set off back to his home. But his wife followed him home, using her magic powers to restore herself to her former self.

The arrival back home of the Sultan's son provoked widespread celebrations in the town and many cannons were fired off. The Sultan's son told his parents about his adventures and the rich man's daughter told her family what she had done. Then she said, "I had better go back and lie in the pit and let my husband come and find me there.

And when the Sultan's son had rested he went to the pit to see how his wife was getting on and he called to her, "Daughter of the Rich man! Daughter of the Rich man!"

And she replied, "I am here." And he called out, "Are you still alive?" And she replied, "Sure, I am still alive. And I have borne you three children while you were away."

"Rubbish!" he shouted. "How can you have borne my three children when I have been married to the daughters of three different Sultans while you have lain all this time in a pit."

After he had left, the Rich Man's daughter went back to her family and asked them to lay on a big feast for her and to invite the Sultan and his family. In the middle of the party the Rich Man's daughter stood up and there was silence. "Now I will tell you what we are celebrating," she said. Then she went outside and returned, bringing her children, each dressed in the clothes of their respective countries of birth, and carrying the gifts their father had given them.

"Go now to your father," she said and they went and sat on the knee of the Sultan's son.

The Sultan's son asked the first child where she was born.

"Muscat," she replied.

"And you?" he asked his son.

"Guava," he replied.

"What about you," he asked his younger daughter.

"I was born in The Land of the Lime Tree," she replied.

"And who is your mother?" he asked them. Each of them pointed at the Rich Man's daughter.

Then the rich man's daughter said, "Did I not say that I would bear you three children?"

And the Sultan's son laughed and admitted, "You have won, daughter of the Rich Man". And they lived together happily ever after.

The Clever Fisherman

There was once a Sultan who lived in the ancient land of Persia. One day he was walking by the sea with his Prime Minister when he came upon a fisherman preparing to cast his line into the sea. The sea was very rough and the wind sang with a high pitched voice.

The Sultan called the fisherman over and said, "Fisherman!" and he replied, "Yes Master."

"Are four and four not enough?" asked the Sultan.

And the fisherman replied, "Four and four are not enough."

And the Sultan said, "Ya Fisherman, Hallah! Hallah!"

And the fisherman said, "Well, I am a very persistent man. I know that there are cuttlefish in here."

The Sultan and his Prime Minister set off on the road back to the town, the Prime Minister scratching his head for he had not understood a word the Sultan and the Fisherman had said.

"Excuse me, Sir...." he began.

"Yes, yes, what is the matter?" asked the Sultan impatiently.

"Could you possibly explain what you were discussing with the fisherman? It sounded just like a riddle to me," said the Prime Minister.

"A high ranking, important Prime Minister ought to understand what a simple fisherman says," replied the Sultan. "If you can't even do that, you are not worthy of your office."

The poor Prime Minister scratched his head harder and thought and thought but in the end he had no choice but to seek out the fisherman and ask him the meaning of the riddle. The fisherman just looked incredulously at the Prime Minister, and said: "Didn't you understand? Do you mean to tell me that you, a high ranking important Prime Minister didn't understand what I, a poor simple fisherman, said?"

The Prime Minister scratched his head even harder and when even that failed to shed any light on the problem, he begged the fisherman to tell him the riddle, promising to pay him a thousand gold coins if he did. But the fisherman just shrugged and turned away.

Then the Prime Minister became even more agitated and offered the fisherman five thousand gold coins, and when he still refused he offered him his house if he would only tell him the answer to the riddle.

"All right, I will explain," said the fisherman. "The 'four and four' to which the Sultan referred were the two parts of the year when there are most fish. The first four are the months when the wind blows from the north; the second four when there are winds of uncertainty and change. These are the months when fishermen fish and save enough for the final four lean months when the wind blows from the south. The Sultan was surprised that I was preparing to fish at a lean time, especially with a storm brewing. What I meant by my reply was that there were not enough fish from the other eight months to last through the summer."

When the Prime Minister heard all this, he went to the Sultan and said, "I have discovered the meaning of what you said to the fisherman." And he told him all that he had discovered.

"How did you persuade him to tell you?" asked the Sultan. When the Prime Minister explained what he had done, and how the fisherman was now living in his house, the Sultan was amazed and summoned the fisherman immediately.

"Why have you done this?" he asked him.

And the fisherman replied, "Well when we met on the coast, and you said "Hallah! Hallah!" I thought you meant, 'Don't give it to him cheaply'. And I answered you, "I am very persistent. I know there are cuttlefish in there," which meant, 'I am a poor man. I know the way to get money.' And so now I am rich. I live in the Prime Minister's house." And when the Sultan saw how his Prime Minister had been cheated, he was furious with him for being such a fool.

"You have been deceived by a humble fisherman," he said to the Prime Minister. "And as you are obviously such a gullible fool, you are of no more use to me. From now on, the fisherman will be my Prime Minister."

And that's how the clever fisherman became Prime Minister and remained so for the rest of his life.

Push Off!

Once, long ago, a poor man named Saleni lived alone in a small house in the village of Malindi. At one time Saleni had been hard-working and prosperous, but when he fell on hard times because he had no sugar to harvest after a long dry season he began borrowing food and money from his neighbours. And when he found how much easier it was to borrow than to work and produce his own food, it became a habit and Saleni became very lazy. So instead of keeping his own chickens to lay eggs, he would simply borrow one from his neighbour Useni, promising to repay it as soon as he could.

Likewise, if he needed flour with which to make his bread, he would go to Joram, who lived across the street and borrow it, again promising to pay it back when he could. Sometimes he even borrowed money to gamble, promising his neighbours that he was guaranteed to win and would be able to pay them back with interest. But his promises were empty ones. He never won at gambling and could never repay his neighbours for any of the items they had lent him.

At last the other villagers became tired of Saleni's borrowing. One by one they knocked on his door demanding repayment but all he would say was, "I have nothing with which to repay you." Sometimes he would add: "But if you lend me some money today, I will bet on a game of cards tonight, and I am bound to win." By now his neighbours had become wise enough to know this was unlikely to happen.

Saleni's neighbours called a meeting to decide what to do about his debts. After much discussion, they decided to take him to Court to try to force him to pay back what he owed them.

When Saleni heard that he had been summoned to Court, he became very worried and went to see his kind neighbour Useni to ask for advice.

"If I tell you what to say, will you promise to repay at least part of my debt after the hearing?" asked Useni.

"Of course," agreed Saleni, anxious to escape prosecution. "When you come to Court, and are asked any question, you must simply reply "Push Off!" advised Useni. "If you say

119

nothing else the Judge will be forced to release you." And so Useni appeared before the Judge.

All his neighbours were in Court as the Judge took his seat among his many advisers. One by one Saleni's neighbours stood up and accused him of not repaying his debts until finally they had all said their piece. The Sultan turned to Saleni and asked, "Is it true what your neighbours have said? Have you borrowed all these items of food and money and not repaid a single one?"

"Push off!" shouted Saleni, as loudly as he could.

"But did you not borrow from any of these people?"

"Push off!" said Saleni again. And no matter what he was asked, the reply was the same: "Push off!"

At last the Judge realised that he was wasting his time asking questions because the answer was always the same. He turned to Saleni's neighbours angrily and asked, "Why do you bring the village idiot before me? It's obvious he doesn't understand a word I am saying or he wouldn't dare speak to me like this. Take him away!"

After Saleni had left the courtroom, his neighbour Useni came quietly up to him and whispered, "You see? It worked. Well done. Now, when will you be able to repay my debt?"

But Saleni just answered, "Push off!"